MW01173667

STORIES BY STEPHEN CAREY FOX

The End of Illusion
The German, 'Mr. Kai' & The Devil
Artists, Thieves & Liars
The Collector
Lou & Billy Joe
The Ghost of Yesterdays
Blame Jason Bourne
A Most Improbable Union
Everybody Knew ... Nobody Knew
The Elephant in the Room

THE ROBIN HOOD SOLUTION

The One Percent and Murder Most Foul

Stephen Carey Fox

The Robin Hood Solution
The One Percent and Murder Most Foul

Cover image: www.ancient-origins.net
Title page image: Adaptation of Robin Hood Movie (2018), Teaser-Trailer.com
Interior image: Hell's Half Acre, by WYDOTman at English Wikipedia, CC BY-SA 3.0, https://commons.wikimedia.org/w/index.php?curid=57295213

ISBN: 979-8872851233

www.mickeysgod.info

Self-styled, 21st century 'Robin Hoods,' angry with wealth inequality, believed their calling was to dispossess the One Percent.

Were these self-proclaimed 'Robin Hoods' the true heirs of Sherwood Forest? True to the legend of the nobleman of Locksley and his Merry Men, a 'motley crew of faithful fugitives,' robbing the rich to help the poor?

If so, how were the heirs of 'Little John,' 'Will Scarlet' and 'Friar Tuck' to transfer stolen wealth to the over-taxed and destitute masses?

Who would play the roles of Prince John and the Sheriff of Nottingham in this 21st century reenactment?

1

Valentine's Day, 2024. Jack's Restaurant, Sausalito, California. Robert Lansing reached across the table and offered his wife Emily a raw oyster. She steadied his hand with hers and slurped the slimy, gray and white mollusk from its half-shell, then closed her eyes and swallowed hard.

They laughed loudly afterward, as though only they occupied the room. Rich people—assuming others will recognize their membership in the one percent and bow to their privileged lifestyle, including their boorish behavior in public—do that.

Robert and Emily appeared to be somewhere between middle age and retirement. They continued to chat amiably but loud still enough to fill the room while they washed down their food with sips of J. Lohr, their favorite Monterey peninsula chardonnay.

The other patrons followed the accepted etiquette and acted as though Robert and Emily didn't exist.

*

In addition to the oysters, their sumptuous spread included Dungeness crab, which took their name from Washington state's sandy Dungeness Spit, which jutted from the Olympic Peninsula into the Strait of Juan de Fuca. The spit sheltered a shallow bay inhabited by the popular delicacy.

Fate, however, was about to leave the couple with no chance to appreciate any of this.

*

Outside, destiny awaited. Two men in their twenties—one could be confident of that based on their slender builds—shivered as they watched the Lansings from behind the corner of a building a half block from Jack's. The air was still heavy with moisture as it had rained for several hours earlier but had now stopped.

"Look at him feed her those oysters!"

"They're both pigs!"

Lansing reached across the table again, and Emily slurped down another ugly mollusk.

"He's preparing for some romance later to-night."

Both men laughed at the reference to the supposed aphrodisiac effect of oysters on the li-bido.

*

The speaker who had the first and last word was Philip Stark, a member of the notorious group whose purported motive was to eliminate eco-nomic inequality by attacking the so-called one percent. The group itself, possibly Marxist but closer to anarchism or nihilism, spoke not by name but by deed: the targeted assassinations of men and women who they believed cared nothing for the down-trodden masses but only the protection and continuation of their own positions of privilege and power.

Set aside the Marxist/nihilist interpretation for the moment. People like Stark were perhaps closer to modern-day, admittedly far more bloodthirsty Robin Hoods, the redistributors of wealth, a 'not-so-merry band' not of Sherwood Forest and the bow, but of Silicon Valley, Wall Street, other bastions of disproportionate wealth, and Glocks, AR-15s, C4, and rocket-propelled grenade launchers,

Lurking with Stark was Ted Powers. Both young men were former students at Brown University, one of many private colleges—this one in Providence, Rhode Island—for the super-smart sons and daughters of the super-rich in the United States. Israel's war to permanently crush Hamas in the Gaza Strip, for which tens of thousands of Palestinians paid with their lives, had radicalized students like Stark and Powers across the country.

Considering their membership in the 'One-Percent Gang' and their purpose that night, the presence of Stark and Powers, both sons of the super-rich like the man they were stalking, represented great irony or hypocrisy—perhaps both. As they gazed at Robert and Emily Lansing wash down their oysters, they could have been watching their own parents.

*

The Lansings had almost reached their parking garage. The night, except for the heavy air, was typical of February in Sausalito, a principal feature of the weather being the fresh, briny smell of the sea. Some found the odor offensive, but not the Lansings.

That smell came, in part, from a sulfur compound called dimethyl sulfide, or DMS, a key player in ocean ecosystems and weather patterns. Scientists had figured out how a particular ocean alga, a single-celled phytoplankton that dwells in the upper sunlit part of the sea, produced the aromatic chemical. The enzyme the algae used to make the compound and the genes that encoded that enzyme, scientists designated Alma1.

Algae used a precursor chemical for protection from the saltiness of its ocean home. Without that chemical, water would rush out of the poor phytoplankton, leading to their salty deaths. The algae converted some of this protective chemical into the smelly stuff, releasing it into the water when the phytoplankton died.

In time, the sulfurous algae emissions escaped into the atmosphere, where beachgoers got the benefit of the familiar smell. That slow seep of emissions was the most abundant source of biological sulfur in the atmosphere; scientists believed it played a major role in controlling the planet's temperature.

*

Excited, thinking or chatting about who could crack a crab the fastest, describing the feeling of an oyster as it slipped down their throats—that superficiality had not, up to then, characterized the relationship between Emily and Robert. They considered themselves, and others did as well, a couple of considerable intellectual depth. Thus, the replay of crabs and oysters as they strolled toward their garage was only the *first* unusual development that night. The second had already begun as the pair arrived at their destination.

The distance of the garage, three blocks from Jack's, had given them time to think and chat about their meal as they approached the neon 'PUBLIC PARKING' sign. The sign, which protruded menacingly over the sidewalk from a concrete façade, beckoned vehicles into the darkened mouth of a multi-level eye sore, its unaesthetic, utilitarian architecture all too familiar to American urbanites.

They took an elevator suffused with stale tobacco smoke up to the 'D' level. Shoppers, late night bargain hunters, had filled every lower level to near capacity. They walked to the spot that faced a concrete wall marked '37' and Robert's sky-blue, Cadillac Escalade, a luxury, full-size SUV.

At first, Robert wasn't sure what he'd seen under the dim fluorescent lighting that bounced off dozens of car roofs as he unlocked both front doors and began to open his. Two masked men wearing dark hoodies to protect their identities from the CCTV cameras found everywhere in metropolitan America walked quietly and calmly up to Emily and Robert, one on each side of the Escalade, and simultaneously shot both in the back of the head.

What Robert wondered he had seen, the last thing he ever saw, was the glint of light off Stark's semi-automatic Glock pistol. If he heard anything, it would have been the discharge of Powers's .45 into his wife's head and the shell casing hitting the cement floor.

Scooping up the shell casings, removing Robert's wallet and Rolex watch and Emily's jewelry, Stark's final move was to pry the keyring from Robert's hand. The killers left the bodies on the garage floor and drove the Escalade down a series of ramps to the toll booth.

Fortunately for the killers, if not justice, Robert had left the parking ticket on top of the center console. Having satisfied the skeptical attendant (two young men driving an expensive Cadillac), the duo exited the garage quickly, before the attendant became more doubtful. Eventually, they found the northbound entrance onto U.S. 101 and from there they continued to a chop-shop familiar to all car thieves in the Bay Area.

*

How did murders like the Lansing's satisfy the One Percenter's goal of wealth redistribution? Simple really. They would use the cash from the sale of their stolen goods—victims' valuables and parts pried loose from vehicles at that chop-shop—to buy the food and medicine they were sure would and alleviate the misery of America's inner cities and the Middle East where perpetual cycles of war victimized millions.

2

Robert Lansing's qualification for membership among the one percent began with a generous bequest from his father of between one and two million dollars. Acting shrewdly and boldly, for that's who he was, Robert grew Edgar Lansing's gift to substantially greater heights in the years ahead.

When interviewed, Robert always maintained that he alone was responsible for his vast holdings, never acknowledging the role played by his father. Without Edgar's safety net, however, Robert never would have had the security necessary to achieve his personal goals. He added to his father's generosity by first investing in equities (stocks and bonds) and then gradually into stock, bond and commodity markets at home and abroad. He reaped additional financial and psychic rewards from a thoroughly different strategy: backing startup companies. Robert Lansing became a venture capitalist.

*

A venture capitalist provided capital from a pool of funds to companies with no access to the equities markets in exchange for an equity stake. Such investors typically targeted firms too risky for banks or capital markets. Recipients might be startups or established companies that wished to expand, companies with strong management teams, a potential market or a unique product or service with a strong competitive advantage. Because venture capitalists sometimes invested in unproven companies, they experienced high rates of failure. For investments that did pan out, the rewards were substantial.

*

The Lansing's home in the City and thus Robert's proximity to Silicon Valley gave him entrée to energetic and creative entrepreneurs eager emulate the success (billions of dollars and international stardom) like Facebook (now Meta), Twitter (X), PayPal and third-party applications for giants like Apple and Microsoft. He very much liked working with and helping to make successes of those young men and women with their flexible minds—American, East Indian and Chinese—bursting with ideas and pouring out of universities like Stanford, MIT, Harvard and California's polytechnic schools.

*

Lansing and others like him needed no further explanation or justification for their achievements than their fidelity to what they loved to call 'free markets.' In truth, but not to their set of truths, the American economy was anything but free.

Since the early 19th century, administration after administration had bent over backwards to ensure the primacy of business by regulating the economy in its favor. They called it *laissez faire* (government *abstention* from interference in the working of the free market), but by definition it was not abstention, or, to put it another way, government abstention would pertain to everyone *but* business.

Whether in French or English, the expression had failed to charm Andrew Jackson in the 1830s. The imbalance of business and the public had grown so skewed he felt obliged to champion the presidency as a bastion of protection for the common man *against* the government's historic bias in favor of the foremost example of big business in 'Old Hickory's day, the Bank of the U.S.

Despite Jackson's short-lived victory over the Bank, until the Roosevelts of the 20th century—Theodore and Franklin—tried to make a difference, the government had continued to regulate the 'free market' economy to the disfavor of American workers.

First came Teddy who railed against the 'malefactors of great wealth': *(Who shall rule this free country—the people through their governmental agents or a few ruthless and domineering men, whose wealth makes them peculiarly formidable, because they hide behind the breastworks of corporate organization).*

Likewise, TR's distant cousin, Franklin, on his war with the 'Liberty League': (*They would squeeze the worker dry in his old age and cast him like an orange rind into the refuse pail*).

Big business invariably cried foul when Congress attempted to regulate it to serve a public interest, but they cheered when lawmakers regulated labor and the public interest to their favor. Regulation, no matter its purpose or who it served or didn't, was not 'freedom.'

Perhaps there was no better example of this inescapable truth than venture capitalism. The law required venture capitalists to follow regulations. Period. Private equity firms and venture capitalists in Lansing's day fell under the regulatory control of the U.S. Securities and Exchange Commission (SEC); banks and other financial institutions had to follow anti-money-laundering regulations.

And did the venture capitalists cry foul? Oh, yes, indeed. Those among them less in tune with political realities spoke aloud from their centuries-old playbook: socialism. In the dead of night, however, those more in tune, and thus more effective and dangerous to the public interest, whispered in barely audible timbres, 'wealth redistribution' and 'over regulation.'

*

The murders of Robert and Emily Lansing stood as a major coup in the opinion and subsequent propaganda of the One Percent Gang. To the businessman's self-righteous killers, who never thought of themselves as 'murderers,' Lansing epitomized the maldistribution of wealth in the United States and beyond, and thus an injustice that only they had the right and the courage to rectify. The authorities and media, on the other hand, refused to call the execution-style deaths of Robert and Emily (she being purely collateral) anything other than cold-blooded murder, and they vowed, of course, as had become the standard promise of law enforcement, to 'bring the murderer or murderers to justice.'

The One Percent Gang. An unequivocally bad idea, or a good idea gone unequivocally catastrophic?

3

Detective Stan O'Neel stood over the bodies of Robert and Emily Lansing and shook his head. His partner, Peter Kenmar was busy testing the bodies and the concrete floor for gun residue, strands of hair—anything the killers might have inadvertently left behind. The coroner had determined the approximate time of death and then spoke briefly with O'Neel.

"Body temps tell me eight to nine o'clock, detective. Probably after dinner. We're not far from Jack's. Have you checked with them?"

"Not yet."

"Any ID?"

"Nothing. Stripped. We'll have to run their prints through our system. Their clothes suggest they had money."

O'Neel told the uniformed sergeant from the Sausalito Police Department to lift the couple's prints.

"You have your kit with you, sergeant?"

"Yes, sir."

Then O'Neel turned to his partner.

"Better run over to Jack's, Peter, and ask about any patrons that left around eight to nine ... Step on it. They may have closed already or are about to close."

"Okay to transport, detective?" the coroner asked.

O'Neel hesitated, turning to Sgt. Fuller.

"You got those prints, sergeant?"

"Yep, all done."

"Alright, Mr. Coroner, you can get 'em out of here. Pretty sh***y place to die."

*

Stan O'Neel and Peter Kenmar had not strayed far from home when they joined the Sausalito Police Department. Both were California boys, through and through, although they came from different backgrounds.

O'Neel's father was a small-town newspaper editor in the Central Valley; Kenmar's a dairy farmer near Ferndale in the northern part of the state. Both were graduates of the state university system. O'Neel had wanted to follow in his father's journalistic footsteps at Chico State but a fascination with police science derailed that plan.

Peter Kenmar, who had enough of milking to last a lifetime, cast his lot locally at College of the Redwoods (also in police science) and finished with a B.A. in political science at Humboldt State. His muscular bulk from all that dairying made him a punishing linebacker on the college's football team.

*

"I'm not sure, detective," the young hostess at Jack's responded to Kenmar's questioning after the detective showed her his shield. He did not explain the reason for his request. He figured her for some college kid.

"You have credit card receipts, don't you?"

"Sure."

"They'll have a signature and time stamp, right?"

"Yes, of course! Why didn't I think of that?"

She opened the register and took out a handful of receipts.

"Better let me look through, those, Miss."

"It's Caldwell, detective. Her tone was anything but deferential. Ms. Julia Caldwell."

Kenmar nodded as he took the receipts. He was tempted to give her a hard time about her tone but decided she was too damn good looking to alienate.

As he thumbed through the receipts, he got flirtatious.

"You go to school around here?"

She wasn't playing along.

"That question got anything to do with why you're here, detective?"

He continued to go through the curled-up tabs without replying. He knew she'd won the skirmish. He didn't mind.

"What about this one? You recognize the writing?"

"No."

"What's the time stamp?"

He was letting her be part of the investigation to a point.

"Seven-sixteen."

"Okay, keep looking."

She picked out several more with time stamps in the range of 8 to 9 PM.

"Print those names so I can read them, okay?"

"I recognize most. They're regulars."

"Keep looking. One that's unusual ... That you don't recognize."

Two minutes passed. Gave him a chance to look her over more carefully. He made some mental notes: height approximately 5'7"; weight approximately 130; blue eyes; brunette; 34B-cup.

She saw what he was doing; she didn't mind.

"Here's one with almost *no* tip."

"Time stamp?"

"Eight-thirty-seven. L-O or A-N or M-S something then ends in G is my guess on the signature ... College of Marin."

She had finally got around to answering his question about school, but he was slow to pick it up.

"Wait, he, she goes to Marin?"

"No! I do. Me, Julie Caldwell."

He pretended to ignore her obvious suggestiveness and the use of her familiar name. She, in turn, blushed, embarrassed at her forwardness.

The mutually flirtatious diversion from the job at hand ended.

"Let me see it," he said.

Kenmar studied the name for a few seconds.

"No, I can't do better than you, but write out the full credit card number. I see it's AMEX. We can run the number and get the name that way."

"You can do that?"

He ignored her. He wasn't going to get into a debate about privacy with her. 'Besides,' he mused, 'she'd probably win that argument.'

"Also, what he, she, they ate," he continued. "Any chance you remember he, she, they?"

"No chance. I'm usually looking down at the paperwork, not up at faces."

"Might be a good idea to start looking up, 'Julie,'" he suggested.

She smiled. He liked it.

4

No part of this extended exchange escaped the attention of Julie's boss, Alan Baker. He waited until the detective left and then approached his employee.

Baker knew his hostess was interested in men. He'd passed it off before as playful flirting when he thought no policeman was involved, but not this time.

"Cop?"

"Yes, a Detective Kenmar. Sausalito police."

"What'd he want?"

"Didn't say specifically... I mean he didn't say *why* he wanted to look at the credit card stubs."

"And you complied?"

"Yes, sir."

"The next time something like that happens wait before proceeding and call me over. Understood?"

"Yes, sir."

Baker felt he needed to make an even stronger impression on his hostess.

"Didn't you know he needed a warrant for something like that? Privacy laws protect credit card information. Did you ask if he had a warrant?"

Julie gulped and blushed.

"No, sir."

"Don't let *that* happen again."

"I'm very sorry, Mr. Baker. You can count on me in the future."

"I'll need to count on you, Julia."

*

Two days later.

"Here's the ME toxicology and stomach content's report, Stan. Both clean, except for alcohol. White wine. Get this! J. Lohr chardonnay."

"You gotta be sh***in' me! They can tell the name of the vintner? And the year?"

"Oh, yeah. 2021. Scary right?"

"Stomach contents?"

"A fine meal of oysters and crab."

"You're holding something back. I can tell by that smirk."

"Yeah, more scary s**t. Farm oysters from Humboldt Bay. Dungeness crab from right here ... Well, five miles off the Golden Gate."

O'Neel shook his head in disbelief, and then continued.

"I've got news for you, my friend. Positive print ID on both deceased: Mr. and Mrs. Robert Lansing. And the wine, oysters and crab came from Jack's Restaurant. Confirmed by credit card receipt. Looks like a mugging gone south for the Lansings. Maybe he resisted. No other motive suggested, so, I'm shutting down the investigation, closing the case ...

"Oh, one more thing. I got a royal chewing out from the boss about your trip to Jack's and a credit card search without a warrant. I'm sorry to say he's gonna dock both our pay. We screwed up."

5

"Detective O'Neel?"

"Yeah."

O'Neel didn't intend to sound impolite or disrespectful, but he was tired and ready to call it a day.

"My name is David Lansing."

O'Neel's senses went to full alert when he heard the name. He didn't know why Lansing had called, but he knew he had to be cautious and speak sympathetically and firmly at the same time.

"I'm told you're leading the investigation into my parents' murders."

"I was. I closed that case."

"Really ... May I ask why?"

"I'm very sorry for your loss, Mr. Lansing, but the only evidence we had pointed to a classic mugging."

"I think you should reopen it."

In Lansing's insistence, O'Neel sensed a tone of disrespect. His distrust of the caller grew.

"And why should I do that?"

"New evidence that's come my way."

O'Neel now had two conflicting views. He didn't like the caller's challenge to his authority, but he was also a policeman and by nature of that occupation, curious.

"I really shouldn't be having this conversation with you, Mr. Lansing, but you've aroused my nosey gene. So, shoot. Let's hear about this 'new' evidence of yours."

O'Neel snapped his fingers to get Kenmar's attention, and then waved at the phone. Kenmar had been taking a statement in another case. He gently picked up his phone, covered the mouthpiece and signaled he was listening.

"I received a phone call," Lansing began hesitantly, choosing his words carefully, "from someone calling himself, 'Mr. Justice.' He claimed to have my father's wallet and cell phone—that's how he got my number—and, he said, unless I released all of my father's financial holdings to him—he didn't explain how that would work—or, and here's the hard part, he'd start killing my family one by one until I complied ... fully."

Kenmar shrugged silently at O'Neel, as if to say he didn't know what to make of the call.

"Whoa! Whoa there, pardner," O'Neel cautioned Lansing. "You telling me your parent's killer, or someone with your father's wallet and cell phone, is threatening your family?"

"I thought I'd made that clear, detective. I'm not sure I'm speaking to the right person. Maybe you should get your supervisor."

After the reprimand O'Neel had just received, to have Lansing go over his head to the boss was the last thing he wanted to happen. He looked at Kenmar, who gave him a blank stare in reply.

"Oh," Lansing chimed in again, "this 'Mr. Justice' warned me not to go to the cops."

Classic extortion, O'Neel thought. He'd need to play hard ball with Lansing.

"Don't threaten me, Mr. Lansing. It will not go well for you. I don't believe we need to bother my super with this for the moment, and I don't want you coming here, as they are probably watching you. They may even be tapping your phone."

"So, you believe me?"

"I do until we get information that says I shouldn't. Are you calling from cell or landline?"

"Cell."

"Do you know what a burner phone is?"

"Burner?"

"Yes, one of those $10 ones you can buy at a supermarket or Walmart. Get one of those and call me back. Each time you believe you need to call me, get a new 'burner' and dispose of the old one. You dispose of them by throwing away the battery or throwing the phone in the river. Otherwise, they can track you. Get rid of your current phone. It's compromised. Goodbye, Mr. Lansing."

O'Neel turned to Kenmar.

"I'm going to the boss. You comin'?

6

"Yeah, yeah, Stan. What now?" the man said impatiently.

That man, Michael Sean Allen, Sausalito's police chief, was a bull of an Irish American. He and his auburn hair—what remained—towered over most everyone at police headquarters. At 6'6" and tipping the scales at 270 to 280, if he hadn't already convinced them of the error of their ways with his piercing hazel eyes that at times appeared to those under him as red-hot coals, he could have squashed all like bugs if he happened to fall on them. And fall on them he did—figuratively.

Chief Allen's family had left the ethnic mix of Cincinnati, Ohio, at the outset of the war in 1941 and headed for the big money in Henry J. Kaiser's California shipyards.

*

Kaiser had started building merchant ships for the U.S. Maritime Commission in 1939. A year later, he established his first Richmond shipyard to help meet Britain's wartime need, and the year after that an additional Richmond yard for Liberty ships.

After Pearl Harbor, he started his third and fourth yards, building troop transports and tank landing ships (LSTs), respectively. Kaiser situated three other yards along the Columbia and Willamette rivers.

Kaiser developed new methods that allowed his yards to outproduce similar facilities. His workers completed ships in two-thirds the time and at a quarter of the cost of all other shipyard averages. The assembly of Liberty ships typically took a little over two weeks; workers—mostly riveters and carpenters—managed to float one in less than five days.

Together, the Kaiser Shipyards produced 747 ships for carrying general cargo and military munitions, armaments and supplies, more than any other complex in the United States.

*

Allen's father, also Michael, prided himself on his contribution to the astonishing turnout of those Liberty ships, ships that ere were destined to carry the sons of millions of other 'Michael Allens,' 'John Aldens' and 'Vincenzo Spataros' to North Africa, Italy, Normandy and dozens of Pacific Islands, the latter made less 'pacific' by their arrival. It was a lesson in the application of democracy, government and private ingenuity, determination, centralized direction and power that Mike junior never allowed those responsible to him to forget.

'Big Mike,' as junior was affectionately known, but never to his face, was anything but a seafaring man. Instead, he attended the requisite police academies and rose quickly through the ranks of the Sausalito PD, having done nearly every job of those under him from beat cop to chief of the detective squad. That body of experience gave him the respect of his officers, a respect that bordered on reverence. Put simply, one did not mess with Mike Allen, not even his plainclothes detectives, and especially detectives he had just reprimanded.

But Chief Allen also had a softer side, doubtless due to the influence of his Quaker mother, Mary. What a pair! Big, loud and energetic Michael and peaceful, prayerful and soft-spoken Mary. Theirs was an American story, perhaps *the* American story, a grasping mythical legend fast approaching extinction.

*

Intimidated but not silenced, Stan O'Neel cautiously laid out what he'd heard from David Lansing.

Mike listened and then blew.

"Guy's a bozo, Stan! Dreams of glory. I thought you knew better than to fall for a stunt like his. Let me make this as simple and clear as I can. I don't want my detectives spending another minute on this BS. You got it? But if you don't get it, I'll find someone who does. *Capeesh*?"

Peter Kenmar had no desire to end up a smashed bug under the chief's heel. He nudged

O'Neel's elbow and signaled the way to the door with a sideways jerk of his head.

O'Neel stood his ground and stared at Chief Allen. He knew that if the Lansing case was as important as he believed, he needed to be more persuasive than ever before.

"All my years on the force have taught me to listen to my gut. You know yourself, Chief, that a lot of police work is instinct, a hunch, and often those hunches lead to getting bad guys off the street."

The chief's look told O'Neel he'd made a point that interested Allen. Before Big Mike could respond, O'Neel continued.

"Tell you what, Chief, before you close out the Lansing case for good, check NI-BRS. I'm sure it includes Marin. If there's nothing there, I'll forget the whole thing. But if you get positive results, we may be onto something big."

*

In January 2021, the FBI's National Incident-Based Reporting System (NI-BRS) became the standard for law enforcement crime data submitted by states and local law enforcement agencies in the United States. The system captured detailed information about the characteristics of crimes: types and amount of property lost; demographic information about victims, offenders, and persons arrested; and what type of weapon, if any, was used in the incident.

NI-BRS covered three-fourths of the U.S. population, serving 119 cities and counties with a population of 250,000 or more: 65.4 million Americans.

*

"What do you imagine the NI-BRS data will show that bears on this case?" Allen asked.

Big Mike appeared to have signaled to O'Neel that he was open to the possibility that murder and extortion elsewhere in the country resembled the Lansing case.

"Copy-cats. All I'm asking, Chief, is to consider the possibility of similar crimes statewide ... perhaps nationwide—of the murder of wealthy people and extortion of their assets by threats to their families. Just look at NI-BRS. That's all I'm asking. If there's nothing there, I'll tell Lansing we're done.

7

Chief Allen was about to discover something that would make him wish he hadn't gone to work that day. NI-BRS revealed crimes in other cities in the United States *like the Lansing case*—murder and extortion. In Hartford, Connecticut, the police referred to the criminals as the 'One-Precent Gang.'

There were hints here and there of the need for law enforcement on the West Coast to organize, but thus far it hadn't happened. No one, no department, bureau or agency had yet attempted to mount a counter offensive. Not even the FBI.

*

"O'Neel! Kenmar! Get in here!"

The two detectives looked at each other in the way only the condemned do, their fates sealed by the chief's tone and volume. Preparing for the worst, both unhitched their pieces and pulled their badges out of jacket pockets. They assumed that's what Allen wanted: reassignment to a desk, administrative leave, demotion or outright dismissal. O'Neel was about to ask Allen's administrative assistant to get their union rep on the phone but thought better of it when he saw Allen's open door.

"Close it behind you, Peter."

Kenmar gave O'Neel that look and shrugged.

'He called me by my first name!' The thought should have pleased him, but he wasn't sure why it didn't.

"You still in touch with that Lansing guy?"

"Not lately, Chief, after you told us to stand down."

Big Mike Allen was not the type to admit to a mistake, easily or otherwise.

'Humph' was all they heard in reply. Then Allen got serious.

"For your information, Detective O'Neel ... and you, too, Kenmar (no more 'Peter') the NIBRS revealed what appeared to be copy-cat cases ... and no one has done a goddamn thing to stop it—them! So, congratulations! You two are going to sound the alarm, run up the flag and we'll see who salutes it."

Kenmar thought the chief sounded like he was about to go to war ... right after he thought Allen was stark, raving mad. He looked at O'Neel who had no interest in acknowledging either possibility. He wasn't wrong.

"So," Allen continued, confirming Kenmar's suspicion, "we need to make war on these guys, and since no one else has stepped up, we're going to do it—*you're* going to do it."

Somewhat to Kenmar's relief, O'Neel finally seemed to snap out of his fog and pay attention to the seriousness of Allen's command. But his meek and unforthcoming reply did not reassure his partner.

"Thanks, boss ... I think."

"You got a problem with what I just said, Stan?"

Kenmar thought he saw Mike's height and weight grow exponentially in that tension-filled moment.

"Of course not, boss," O'Neel responded more forcefully.

"Okay, then. I've had enough of this. You two get out of here and get me some bad guys, *Capeesh*?"

On their way to the door, Kenmar wondered why the chief sometimes used language from movies about the Mafia—the Mob. Was it a sign of respect or derision?

8

Eighteen months earlier. Dawn. Arco, Idaho, a town of about 900 in Butte County on the Big Lost River northeast of Craters of the Moon National Monument.

A youngish looking man stepped out of the last room in a short row of rooms at the Lost River Motel. Shivering in the early morning cool, he lit a cigarette, thinking perhaps it would warm him but was more likely a sign of addiction.

Minutes later a pickup truck, a nine or ten-year-old Ford 150, pulled into the parking lot and the driver stopped in front of Number 4 next to a six-year-old Ram 1500. He got out, waved and walked over to the man from Number 5. They embraced, as old friends would.

*

For blocks around the motel, grass and weeds grew out of cracks in the concrete foundations and slabs of what had once been homes or businesses.

"This was once an interesting place," the Ram 1500 said to the Ford 150. "The town's first name was 'Root Hog,' but it was then located five miles south of here."

"Really? Root Hog?"

"Yeah, apparently, the town leaders, tired of people making fun of 'Root Hog,' applied to the U.S. Post Office for the town name of 'Junction,' but the Postmaster General thought that name too common."

"No!"

"Yeah, then the general got a little crazy and suggested the name, 'Arco,' after Georg von Arco, a German visiting Washington at the time."

"That's nuts!"

"Von Arco, who died in 1940, was an inventor and a pioneer in the field of radio transmission. He became the lead engineer for a company that produced radio vacuum tubes ...

"When the railroad came, the town of Arco moved up here. You see that rocky hill over there, with numbers painted all over it?"

"Yeah."

"The local high school has a tradition of each class since 1920 painting its graduation year on the face of hill."

"And how did you come by all this 'wisdom'?"

"The motel manager. Guess he doesn't get many guests, so he picked me for the trip down history lane."

"Right up your alley," the Ford 150 man said.

"Yeah, but maybe the most interesting thing he told me was this: for about an hour in July 1955, Arco was the first community in the world electrified entirely and solely by nuclear power!"

*

Ayman Robinson, the man from Room 5 and the driver of the Ram 1500, an undergraduate *cum laude* of the University of California (Berkeley) and graduate *cum laude* of the University of Michigan with degrees in history and economics, and currently on parole from the state's premier prison, appeared to be of average height and weight for a man in his late twenties. His thick dark hair, which nonetheless showed the first signs of male pattern baldness stirred in a light morning breeze.

A superior court judge in Ann Arbor had sentenced him to five years after a jury found him guilty of participation in a campus riot that resulted in a conflagration and destruction of two buildings associated with the economics and business schools. In court, Robinson justified his actions to have been against what he called 'a system that perpetuated gross income inequality.'

Evidence convinced the jury of the truth of his defense, but the 12 men and women did not believe it justified his actions that night. Robinson remained unrepentant and unremorseful as the marshals led him away after the verdict.

His destination: the Parnall Correctional Facility in Jackson, Jackson County, Michigan, one portion of the former Michigan State Prison that operated by the Michigan Department of

Corrections since 1926. At the time of extensive rioting that rocked the 'joint' in the early 1980s, Parnall was the largest walled prison in the world.

In prison, Robinson began to pen a manifesto destined to become what he called a new declaration of independence. He believed, as all dreamers and schemers do, men like John Brown or Adolf Hitler, that his words of righteous anger would rally citizens across the country in a crusade against income inequality and other oppressions. And, as other notable crusades had, Robinson's came to rely on any means necessary to achieve his aims: theft, extortion—even murder. He would become the co-founder of that 'One-Percent Gang.'

The other founder, the man from the Ford 150 embracing Robinson amid the desolation of a once thriving town, was Drew Hainey of Detroit, a graduate with honors of the U of M but in political science and philosophy. The two men, embracing and smiling as the sun began to peep over the horizon, had done time together at Parnall for the same crime—the destructive campus riot.

Cum laude and 'with honors.' Who could not accept their righteous truths?

*

Did the two men hang out together at Michigan? There was little direct evidence they did until their senior year, but one must assume they had to have done so. Neither man showed any interest in women at Michigan. Were they gay? There was speculation of such a relationship among those who knew them at Michigan and Parnall, although they had few friends, but again no evidence. A better argument that might be put forward was that they only came to know each other at Parnall. The most confident thing that could be said of the pair was that they worked together at Parnall. The rest would have to remain enigmatic.

*

As Robinson scribbled out hand-written pages of his manifesto, a sympathetic Parnall guard slipped them to Hainey who edited them with an eye to perfecting an unassailable explication of their political and philosophical ideas.

That the final manifesto read like Thomas Jefferson's Declaration was no accident. Jefferson's accusations against the king translated into Robinson and Hainey's personal grievances, plus those they directed at the worst excesses of capitalism.

9

Ayman Robinson and Drew Hainey's manifesto, their *New 'Declaration of Independence,'* laid out their premises and solutions, their Whereases and Resolves. Robinson and Hainey had adopted a *New 'Robin Hood' Solution*: take from the rich and give to the poor.

A Renewed 'Declaration of Independence'

Whereas: *Income and wealth inequality in the United States is substantially higher and outpacing almost any other developed nation.* The 2008 global financial crisis, the slow and uneven recovery, and the economic shock caused by the COVID-19 pandemic have only deepened that trend. Meanwhile, a boom in stock and home prices primarily benefited wealthy Americans who owned more of those assets.

Whereas: *Economists say the causes of worsening inequality could weaken democracy and give rise to authoritarian movements.* Those causes were: 1) failure to adapt to globalization and technological change; 2) shifting tax policy; 3) reduced bargaining power among workers; 4) and long-standing racial and gender discrimination.

Whereas: *The incomes of the highest echelon of earners, the one percent, are rapidly outpacing the rest of the population.* The picture is much the same when looking total net worth rather than yearly income.

Whereas: *There are signs that economic mobility, lower in the United States than in many other developed countries, is disappearing.* Black and American Indian children have far lower economic mobility compared to white, Asian and children of Hispanic ethnicity.

Whereas: *The relationship between race, ethnicity and inequality had been well-documented.* Since 1960, the median wealth of white households has tripled while the wealth of Black households had barely increased. For decades, the unemployment rate among Black Americans has been roughly twice that of white Americans. Black Americans are underrepresented in high-paying professions, including corporate leadership.

Whereas: *Wealth inequality is rooted in systemic racism and the legacy of slavery.* Black Americans are systematically denied mortgages, leading to housing segregation and a disparity in home ownership, which is a major source of wealth.

Whereas: *Black Americans face discrimination in the labor market.* Hiring is often done internally via networks that exclude them.

Whereas: *Most high wages come from jobs that require a high level of education.* Households with a bachelor's degree earn twice those headed by someone without. Families with a postgraduate degree holder earn nearly three times as much. Families headed by a postgraduate degree holder had nearly eight times more wealth than families without a college degree.

Whereas: *College degrees do not guarantee good jobs.* The Federal Reserve study found that the college wealth premium (the increase in net worth from having a degree) had declined significantly for white Americans born in the 1980s and had disappeared entirely for Black Americans born that decade.

Whereas: *The top U.S. income tax rates have been repeatedly cut over the past half century.* Some experts say this has contributed to growing inequality. The top one percent's share of income dramatically increased after President Ronald Reagan slashed taxes in the early 1980s.

Whereas: *The corporate income tax has declined steadily as a share of corporate profits and as a percentage of gross domestic product over the past half century.*

Whereas: *The capital gains tax has also declined over time.* The wealthy generally benefit more from capital gains than from regular employment income. The gap between the capital gains tax and the income tax contributes to inequality.

Whereas: *Some Americans have greatly benefited from a globalized world.* They can reach more consumers and manufacture products at lower costs. But globalization has also introduced tough competition for American workers, as some jobs have moved overseas and wages have stagnated.

Whereas: *The decline of unions is another contributing factor to economic inequality.* The average union member earns roughly 25 percent more than their non-union counterpart. In 1983 one union represented about 20 percent of all workers. By 2019, that number had dropped to just 6.2 percent.

*

Resolved: *One tool for addressing income inequality that has received significant attention is a more progressive tax code.* Congress should tax higher incomes at a higher rate than lower ones. Congress should dramatically expand access to tax-advantaged retirement savings accounts with proven wealth-building vehicles like the federal Thrift Savings Plan.

Resolved: *Taxes on wealth and inherited wealth should replace taxes on income.*

Resolved: *To address the rising cost of college and increase access to higher education, Congress pass legislation instituting tuition-free public college and the elimination of student loan debt.*

Resolved: *A dynamic economy— an economy experiencing prolonged and robust* *economic growth and a tight labor market and one which encourages entrepreneurialism, worker mobility is unrestricted, and technological innovation is embraced—is good for American workers.*

Resolved: *Persistently high-poverty neighborhoods traps millions of Americans.* The United States needs a robust, place-based policy agenda to support residents of struggling communities and regions.

Ayman Hamouda-Robinson

Drew Hainey

*

The authors, whose egos trumped any suggestion of good sense, believed they needed to rally public opinion behind their manifesto and themselves personally should the public view their actions as extreme, in which case they'd need protection. Such minds usually find a way or ways to rationalize aberrant and abhorrent behavior. So, in their defense they created a website and published the declaration. It was as much a warning as a declaration.

10

Ayman Robinson's father was Albert, whose roots lay in the Black belt of Alabama. Ayman's mother, Aisha Hamouda, was Palestinian. Her family had joined the forced refugee diaspora after 1948. Robinson's maternal grandparents realized they would never have a place in the new state of Israel, nor did the overcrowded camps of Jordan, Syria, Lebanon and the Gaza Strip hold much appeal. But what choice did they have?

Dreamers among the Palestinians remained to fight for their homeland; for the sake of their children, Sami and Jamila Hamouda did not. They chose instead the United States.

Albert Robinson, whose family was part of the great Black migration out of the South in the early decades of he 20th century, and Aisha Hamouda met and dated in high school. Albert wasn't much of a student, and the jobs he held or couldn't hold after high school showed him incapable of supporting his family. Aisha woke one Sunday morning to an empty bed. Albert had fled in shame and vanished forever from his Detroit family.

Aisha took her two children, Ayman and Aya, in her arms and explained if they were to survive the mean streets of Detroit and flourish, they would need to study and work hard.

*

Drew Hainey, as one might have guessed already, was of Irish and English descent. Like the Robinson's, Mary Whelan and Seamus Hainey met in high school. As often happened before the pill, when young lovers yearned for each other in the way only marriage could satisfy, the predictable reality of Drew, growing in his mother's belly, precluded Mary's dream of a normal Catholic wedding, even in Woodward Avenue's Cathedral of the Most Blessed Sacrament. Instead, she and Seamus rushed to a downtown wedding chapel and took their vows in the parlor of a Filipino Elvis impersonator.

A few lean years and innumerable pints later, Seamus realized he wasn't ready for the responsibilities of husband and father and, perhaps also on a Sunday, he fled to his sea-going roots. After an absence of two years, he wrote to Mary once or twice from the Old Sod, then disappeared, perhaps drowned.

Mary hadn't waited for those letters to take young Drew in her arms, as Mona had Ayman, and set before him the same challenge: work and study hard if you want to be heard in this place.

Ayman and Drew worked hard. They were fortunate to have teachers who recognized promise when they saw it. High test scores and an admissions staff at the University of Michigan, who also recognized promise and that boys from the mean streets of Detroit deserved a chance.

*

Why did that promise become murderous? What environment—or environments—what thinking would cause two highly intelligent, honored graduates of a premier learning institution to become zealous and ruthless agents against the system that had opened doors for them, crusaders whose tactics mimicked Mob bosses?

Take Detroit, the hometown of both men. Not the Detroit of Grosse Point or of middle-class neighborhoods, but of impoverished Fiskhorn and Poletown East. Ayman and Drew's discontent began there with awful statistics.

Real estate exceptionally low. Per capita income exceptionally low. Childhood poverty exceptionally high. Two-thirds of Fiskhorn's children lived in poverty.

Then there were the exceptionally high number of households headed by single mothers, households like the Robinson's and Hainey's. It should surprise no one those children from single parent households, weighted down by poverty and, importantly, low-weight births and infant mortality, were more likely to commit crimes—particularly violent crime.

*

The Poletown East neighborhood emerged as part of Detroit in the 1870s with the first waves of Polish immigrants. It served as the heart of Detroit's Polish community for many years.

Few among Detroit's political and powerful elites took the people of Poletown East seriously. In 1981, the city demolished a portion of the neighborhood to make way for an automobile assembly plant. General Motors and the cities of Detroit and Hamtramck relied on eminent domain to relocate 4,200 people from Poletown East.

*

Why did the promise of Ayman and Drew go wrong? One could legitimately argue it went wrong when those young men were born. It went wrong when no one cared enough about impoverished neighborhoods, when no one cared enough about childhood poverty, when no one cared enough about crime, when the residents of Poletown East had no political clout to protect them from ambitious politicians and investors in General Motors stock.

It went wrong when the United States turned its back on Palestinians. It went wrong when banks refused loans to bright boys who had good ideas for startups but couldn't move investors like Robert Lansing to see beyond the mean streets of Detroit. It went wrong when institutions like the University of Michigan believed their responsibility for the above ended at the admission's office door.

*

Yes, there was plenty of wrong. Someone had their foot on the necks of stateless Palestinians and the Micks and Pollocks of Fiskhorn and Poletown East and wouldn't lift it. Someone had to remove that foot.

But when did removing that foot turn sociopathic and psychopathic? Thousands of young men emerged from that environment and didn't become sociopathic or psychopathic.

When did it become the sole responsibility of two graduates of the University of Michigan to right with violence the wrongs *they* perceived? Had their courses radicalized them?

What turned them away from legitimate efforts to ameliorate toward murderous insanity?

What turned brilliant minds turned into vessels of amorality in which murder was no longer murder? When murder became just another arrow in the quiver of righteousness? A quiver of righteousness that belonged exclusively to two megalomaniacal young men.

No one can say with certainty they know the precise trigger or triggers, and thus society was robbed of the chance to prevent a repetition or repetitions.

*

The meeting that chilly morning in a town once entirely lit by nuclear power, was also the seed for a broad effort to recruit and vet dedicated and loyal followers who would become members of differential cells whose bitterness, fanaticism and violent temperaments would be the hallmarks of the 'gang.' Philip Stark and Ted Powers belonged to one of those cells.

Hamouda-Robinson (Ayman had decided to link his mother's family name to his father's to acknowledge the Palestinians' struggle but will be simply Hamouda ahead) and Hainey were mindful of history. At U of M and Parnall they had studied anarchists and revolutionaries in Russia, Ireland, France, Germany, and Switzerland, which had adopted cell organization in the 1880s, as did the communist movement in the late 19th century. They did so because highly organized and determined cells are remarkably difficult for foes to penetrate.

The Arco pair decided their cell organization, whether specialized or ad hoc, must follow a cardinal principle: compartmentalize information based on 'need to know' no matter the cell's role. That would allow the organization to survive if opponents compromised one of the cells.

Hamouda and Hainey decided to rely on three types of cells. Support cells to provide drivers' licenses, cash, credit cards, or lodging and, if appropriate, bomb building materials.

Sleeper cells, staffed by those who may have lived in the target area for some time, Sausalito, for example, would do nothing until activated.

The final stages of activation and attack fell to execution cells, to men like Stark and Powers, who would utilize the other cells' contributions.

Overall command, the job of coordinating and focusing all the cells, belonged to the most highly educated, to men like Hamouda-Robinson and Hainey.

The Arco duo communicated to all their cells via encrypted messages written and distributed to assets nationwide by a trusted colleague—trusted without reservation. Their hides depended on it.

11

"You fellas read this crap, this new 'Declaration of Independence'? I get they're pissed at the one percent, but could that cause those bozos to kill? And kill in *my* jurisdiction! ...

"I think after reading that manifesto, we can safely assume they killed Lansing because of his having big bucks and history as a venture capitalist, and what his son claimed about the threatened extortion by this 'Mr. Justice.' But I want *solid* answers. I want the dots connected, and I want it done fast! *Capeesh*? ...

"Oh, I almost forgot. Have you finished setting up the 'round-the-clock protection for the Lansing kid and his family?"

Detectives O'Neel and Kenmar looked at each other in ways that suggested they didn't get the depth of their boss's anger, his personalization of the Lansing killings, and for the moment they hadn't a clue how to find the answer Big Mike wanted about the killers. They did, however, give him a satisfactory answer about the protection they'd set up for David Lansing.

As they left his office, their hides barely intact, O'Neel suggested a starting point from which they might begin to satisfy Allen's demands.

"I think we should have heart-to-heart with Mr. David Lansing. We've got to figure out why they killed his father and mother. Was it the one percent thing? It would help, of course, if we knew who the killers were. Was the hit planned or just an opportunity? The threatened extortion leads me to believe someone planned it, and that someone either did it himself or had others do it."

*

David Lansing picked up his phone.

"Who's calling?" he said hesitantly.

"Detective O'Neel of the Sausalito Police Department. We spoke earlier about your choice of phones."

"Ah, yes, I remember."

"Are you using a burner right now?"

"I think so. I bought it at Walmart."

"What did it cost?"

"Fifteen dollars."

"Good. Now, I'm going to send an unmarked vehicle to the public library parking lot. I want you to go to the library with your phone and wait for further instructions. Do you understand?"

"Yes."

*

Thirty minutes later.

"Mr. Lansing?"

"Yes?"

"Do you see a dark gray van in the last row of cars?"

"I think so."

"I want you to walk to that van. When you get close, the door will slide open. Climb in. I am inside."

David Lansing did as instructed.

The two men shook hands, and O'Neel offered Lansing a seat. The electronics that occupied most of the van impressed Lansing. He'd seen similar set ups in movies, but this was the real thing.

"Do you think you were followed?"

"I'm not sure. I don't think so. How does one know?"

O'Neel decided Lansing's question would consume time and detract from the purpose of the clandestine meeting.

"I can't explain that now, Mr. Lansing, so, I'll come straight to the point. I want you to think hard. Do you remember anything your father did or said that would cause people to want him dead? Did he have enemies? Maybe something to do with his investments in startups."

"Well, people like my father are bound to have made some enemies, but no, nothing and no one comes to mind. As for money, with startups there are always winners and losers. But murder? I couldn't ... can't imagine competition for his money going to such an extreme."

“Did he ever share details of his business activities or associates with the family?”

“Not with me. Maybe my mother, but I had no way of knowing about that.”

“Okay. We appreciate your cooperation. You can go but continue to practice the cautions we’ve discussed.”

*

O’Neel and Kenmar sat in one of the department’s squad rooms. O’Neel briefed his partner on his meeting with David Lansing.

“I don’t know, Stan. I think he’s gonna get burned. He doesn’t seem to get why he needs to be careful ...

“Changing the subject, I have a suggestion for our way forward.”

“Good! Shoot. I’m tired of Lansing.”

“Let’s learn all we can about Hamouda and Hainey, concentrating on whether they had any direct or indirect connection to Lansing.”

O’Neel readily agreed, and they went to Chief Allen, hoping to enlist his support.

He agreed to their plan and requested the rap sheets on both men from the Ann Arbor Police Department and Parnall.

The trio decided to contact the men's professors at Michigan and Parnall's warden. O'Neel would go to Ann Arbor and Kenmar to Jackson. Michigan. Allen sat back after doing what a boss is supposed to do—provide direction and support.

*

Kenmar had better luck than O'Neel, luck of a quality neither man could have imagined. The Parnall files on Hainey and Hamouda included the names and addresses of all their correspondents! It was the first breakthrough in the case.

"Anything at Michigan?" Kenmar asked O'Neel when they met two days later at O'Neel's hotel in Ann Arbor.

"Nah, dry hole. The faculty, some of them, anyway, were overly suspicious of me and held back. The really liberal ones. I could sense it. You'd like to think murder would shake them loose a little, but no. How'd you make out?"

"I think I found something. They made me a copy of all Hainey and Hamouda's correspondence," Kenmar reported.

O'Neel, who had been lounging in a soft chair, shot to his feet.

"That's fantastic, Peter! Let's check those names against the ones believed to have been victims of the gang. Then, we'll do the same against the FBI's list of folks with similar MOs, especially those in Michigan."

When they had finished days later, they had no matches with murder victims, but four names that seemed to fit the detectives' filters surfaced during their examination of FBI files. They found the same four in the Parnall correspondence: Brian Downing, Theodore Powers, Alton Rogers and Philip Stark. Moreover, two of those men had Post Office boxes.

"Holy shit! Peter. Stark lives in Petaluma, either that or he just collects his mail there, and Powers in Santa Rosa. Same issue with his address."

"But who are Downing and Rogers? Why no addresses for them? Does that mean we have four suspects in the Lansing killings?"

"Look, all we know is that these four appeared on a list of correspondents, and they match names the FBI has for whatever reason. They could also be potential victims."

"I don't believe anyone writing to someone at Parnall would be a victim or potential victim. No, we must assume these guys are members of the gang. I can't imagine Robert Lansing having any reason to know such people or write to them.

"Good point, Stan. I agree. Let's take it to the boss and see what he wants to do about it."

12

Big Mike Allen also dismissed the idea that the four were potential victims. He wanted his detectives to focus on them as murder suspects. It did puzzle Allen, however, that the FBI hadn't already gone after them.

"Best guess," O'Neel said, "they didn't bother to obtain their addresses from the prison correspondence."

"Lazy bastards," Big Mike added in disgust. "On the other hand, good police work by you two! ...

"Okay, listen up. All we have are names; we don't have a crime. Their addresses and correspondence with the 'manifesto bozos' make them suspect, but for now that's it."

"Is there enough for probable cause, Chief?"

"It *might* qualify for probable cause, Peter, but Fred Holmes—we'd have to get anything in the way of phone taps and bank records from him—is a real stickler of a judge when it comes to the Constitution. I think we're going to need an overt act or something leaning heavily in the direction of an overt act."

"You mean we wait until they've knocked off someone else?"

Big Mike gave Kenmar a withering stare.

"Come on, Peter. You ought to know me better than that. You know that's *not* what I said. Let's set up the usual surveillance, 12/7 and perimeter."

"You think we can we get a tap, Chief?"

Mike Allen gave O'Neel that same withering stare.

"For Chris sakes, Stan! Pay attention! A tap takes us right back to probable cause! I'm going to have a chat with Judge Holmes about how much rope he'll give us ... maybe a tap, but I doubt it."

While Big Mike Allen met with Judge Holmes, O'Neel and Kenmar started with the low-hanging fruit and arranged for the surveillance of Powers and Stark in Petaluma and Santa Rosa.

*

Chief Allen had misjudged the FBI. The Bureau had not given up on people in the Parnall correspondence in their files. Stark and Powers. They were not so lazy as Allen thought. They, too, had looked at the Parnall correspondence index, long before Detective Kenmar, and saw the connection to Hamouda and Hainey. They simply did not want to share what they had learned with an unfamiliar and, in their view, untested local jurisdiction. Moreover, Bureau regulations forbid it.

Subsequent weeks of FBI surveillance showed that neither Powers nor Stark had attended his mailbox. Did this mean they had become suspicious and left the area?

Neither. Through the eyes of their principal go-between, Hamouda and Hainey watched from a safe distance law enforcement's interest in Stark and Powers. First, the FBI's trip to Parnall and then the Sausalito Police Department's. It seemed clear to the Arco duo that Stark and Powers had become liabilities who had the potential to tie the two leaders to a murder conspiracy.

13

For two men responsible for the heinous murders of Robert and Emily Lansing, Philip Stark and Ted Powers spent too much time together after the executions. Their bar hopping/whoring routine, spread throughout the Bay Area but partial to the peninsula south of the City, took up nearly every weekend night. But they were rank amateurs in the murder for hire business—not in carrying out the executions but in their behavior afterward—two early, hasty and young recruits.

The Lansing killers' liability seemed never to have occurred to them. That was also part of their amateur status. Was the drunken whoring indicative of an awareness of their liability, to have as much fun as possible before the end? Or to consciences that needed salving? Did they not see the ruthlessness of their employers when assigned to carry out the Arco duo's bidding? Were Stark and Powers even capable of entertaining such questions?

*

Shirley Thomas slid into the booth next to Ted Powers. On the bench opposite, her pal Linda Harris sat next to Philip Stark. Shirley tenderly stroked Ted's thigh. His breathing escalated into a series of sighs. Stark's breathing suggested he was likely getting the same attention from Linda.

A look of either woman would surprise no one; subtlety was not their strong suit. Dyed hair, pink or blonde, heavy eye makeup, the same for facial makeup, long fingernails painted to match the hair, or as a contrast, and low-cut tops—

brassiere or not—to showcase décolletage shaded for emphasis.

As the women sat scooched up against their 'dates,' one was left to imagine the length of their skirts, the presence of panties—or not—or tight slacks stretched against prominent buttocks and outlining the crotch as if everything below the waist had been poured in.

The heavy breathing led to more orders of Seven and Sevens for the men and tea to look like bourbon or whiskey for the women.

"Whatcha do, honey?" Shirley asked, nuzzling against Powers's neck, tickling it with blinking fake eyelashes.

"I f**k all day and night. That give you any ideas, 'honey'?"

"Hey! I'm just trying to get to know you, whether you're gonna f**k me tonight. Maybe you ain't, smart-ass!"

Powers grew silent.

"Maybe it's time to go somewhere else, Shirley suggested. We got a nice hotel room ... I mean each of us has a room."

Neither man was sober enough to agree or object.

"Come on, honey," Linda said, dragging Stark out of their booth.

"Hey," Stark said, suddenly aware of the proceedings, "that sounds peachy."

It was anything but 'peachy.'

*

Emergency services in Santa Rosa, California, was a bureaucratic nightmare. The EMS (Emergency Medical Services) Division Chief, who reported to the Deputy Fire Chief of Operations, managed the Emergency Medical Services Division of the fire department. Additionally, each of the three eight-hour shifts had a Field Training Officer (FTO) who directly interacted with the paramedics daily.

The Santa Rosa Fire Department trained all its personnel to the Emergency Medical Technician (EMT) level, and, as paramedics, each was capable of advanced life support techniques. They were also clever enough as well as trained enough to know how to provide the opposite of life support.

*

"Hey, Brad."

"Yo! What's up?"

Can you change your shift tonight? Boss has a job for us."

Brad Coleman and Nick Forrest earned more than a decent five-figure salary as EMTs in the Santa Rosa Fire Department. They were the kind of guys in their early thirties who easily met the requirements of the job: clean driving and criminal records; good physical condition; the ability to remain calm while under stress; the ability to work as part of a team; and the ability to follow orders ... Yes, following orders. But whose?

*

For their protection and to carry out actions that no one could trace to them, Hamouda and Hainey had vetted and recruited a security detail that consisted of men and women like Shirley and Linda, who knew how to exploit human weakness, and Brad and Nick to clean it all up.

The night in question, following the hour or so that began in the booth and, under the FBI's nose, Shirley and Linda lured Stark and Powers into separate hotel rooms in Santa Rosa, where they slipped knockout pills, either choral hydrate or emetic tartar into the men's Seven and Seven's.

With their victims unconscious on beds, they exited the rooms to allow Brad and Nick to do their part. Each of the highly trained EMTs entered one of the rooms. When they left, Stark and Powers were dead.

They transported the bodies to an automobile junk yard and loaded each into a derelict vehicle that appeared ready for the compactor.

*

Two days later the FBI field office in San Francisco received a call from a man identifying himself as the owner of a car junk yard.

"My name is Schafer. I own a car graveyard in Santa Rosa ..."

The switchboard cut him off.

"How should I direct you? What is he nature of our call?"

"I guess I want to report a couple of murders."

"One moment."

Half a minute later.

"Special Agent Wilson. To whom am I speaking?"

"Like I told the operator, my name is Schafer, Tom Schafer, and I own Schafer Auto Junk in Santa Rosa. I already talked to the police department here, but they passed me off to you."

"What is the nature of the police matter?"

"My guys found two bodies in derelicts just before we loaded 'em in the compactor."

"Dead bodies?"

"Stinkin' dead. Two males. Someone broke in here and stuffed 'em into those cars."

"Approximate age?"

"Who me? None of your damn business!"

"No, sir. I apologize. How old would you say the deceased were?"

"Young guys. Mid to late twenties. They sure as hell ain't dead from what you guys call 'natural causes.'"

"Thank you for reporting these deaths. Someone will be in touch shortly."

"Okay ... Thanks ... I guess."

14

"Chief," Darlene interrupted over the intercom, "I've got the FBI on one for you."

"Thanks, Honey," he replied casually.

That Allen called his assistant, 'Honey,' didn't mean what some would say it meant (sexual harassment, misogyny). He never used that term of endearment in public, and, presumably, it didn't offend Darlene. Had he asked her? Unknown. Perhaps he thought of all the women in his command as, 'Honey.'" But the chief wasn't the sort of boss to worry about what people would think or say, even in a hyper-liberal community like Sausalito. He was, after all, '*Big* Mike.'

*

"Chief Allen, Mike Allen?" the voice at the other end of the line inquired.

"That'd be me."

"Special Agent Tom Wilson of the San Francisco filed office."

Allen's senses went to full alert. As far as he was concerned, any contact from the Bureau meant they wanted something without offering anything in return.

Wilson came straight to the point.

"You lose track of a couple of guys named Stark and Powers?"

Big Mike wanted to shout 'YES!' but decided to play it a bit cooler. It *was* the FBI on the other end.

He covered the phone speaker and through the intercom told Darlene to get hold of O'Neel and Kenmar *toute suite*.

Still playing it cool, he asked Wilson to repeat the names.

"They're dead. From their prints we decided to look through NI-BRS. Seems you were once curious about them ... according to the system."

"Yes, those names do sound familiar." Allen was now playing it too cool.

"Look, Chief, let's cut the crap! I don't have all day for games. Either you are or are not interested in the information I have."

"My apologies, agent, I was trying to get my files on-screen when you were talking. Yes. We are definitely interested in your information. You say they're deceased?"

"That's what I said. A guy at a junk car lot found 'em in a couple of cars headed for the compactor. Called us. We got their prints, and you know the rest. What was your interest in them?"

"Long story short, they are prime suspects in an unsolved double execution hit up here. The Lansings."

"Right, got it. Why are they suspects?"

"We connected them to the Hamouda/Hainey 'Declaration.' You familiar with that?"

"Who isn't? ... Ah-Ha! Now I know the case you're talking about. Hamouda and Hainey corresponded with Stark and Powers when the former were in prison in Michigan. Soooo ... You think Hamouda and Hainey sanctioned the hit on the Lansings because of his being among the one percent. Because of that declaration."

Allen sensed his control of the case was slipping from his grasp.

"Yeah, that's about it."

Big Mike's resignation dripped from every word. Seldom had a mere conversation reduced a man of his physical size to such despair so easily.

By then, O'Neel and Kenmar had walked into Allen's office. He waved them toward chairs.

"Look, Chief," Wilson continued, "we're short on manpower here for the moment ..."

Big Mike lit up.

"Would you be interested in working the case up there and keep us abreast of any developments? Of course, we'd need to authorize everything you do; for example, passing along locations, surveillance, taps, search warrants, and so forth. *Comprénde*?"

"I understand, Agent Wilson. May I get back to you later today?"

He wanted to reply in Spanish because he knew Wilson's use of it was a snub.

"Better make it no more than two hours, Chief, or I'll have or rethink my options."

Big Mike was no dummy. He was, in fact, a fair poker player, and he knew a bluff when he saw one—or, in this case, heard one. He knew Wilson had no other 'options.' He found it exhilarating to have the FBI by the short hairs. His earlier despair had vanished in seconds. He smiled broadly at his two detectives.

15

"Stark and Powers are dead," Allen told his stunned detectives.

"What!" they exclaimed in unison.

"Yeah, somebody iced 'em. The guys at a junk car yard in Santa Rosa were about to load some wrecks into the compactor when they saw the bodies inside. The Bureau wants us to assist with the case. I said I'd think it over ...

"Listen. Get up there, grab those bodies and bring 'em back here so the ME can go over 'em with a fine-tooth comb. Use one of the vans. I'll tell the motor pool to add a couple of stretchers ...

"Before you leave, get an authorization from legal to seize the bodies and then move before the FBI changes its mind. While you're gone, I'll put out an APB on Hamouda and Hainey and add what we've learned to the NI-BRS."

"Christ, Chief! You're movin' pretty fast on this."

"Well, to stay ahead of the feds you must. So, I'm gonna accept Wilson's 'generous' offer for us to handle the case. He laid down a bunch of stipulations about checking in with them, but that was all meaningless bull. They always pretend you're useful, and then they grab your stuff so they can preen before the cameras ... hog the headlines. Glory boys."

*

"They're still out there, just where we found 'em. Ain't touched a thing, except a dab of paint on each car so you could find 'em more easily. I always wanna be on the right side of the law.

Don't know what killed 'em; couldn't see a mark on 'em."

"Thanks, Mr. ... Uh, Mr. ...?"

O'Neel struggled for the man's name.

"Schafer, Tom Schafer. I own the place. Got it from my Daddy."

"Yes, well there's a lot of *that* happening these days. We'll take it from here, Mr. Schafer."

"He's gone now ... my Daddy."

"That, too," Kenmar added, but that second bit of sarcasm sailed right over Schafer's head.

*

After the detectives returned with the bodies of Stark and Powers and turned them over to the county medical examiner, Big Mike called them into his office. He was as white as a ghost.

"You okay, boss?" O'Neel said. "You don't look so hot."

"No, I'm not okay. Sit down, both of you." O'Neel and Kenmar looked at each other. They didn't need to shrug. The looks said it all.

"David Lansing is dead. He and his whole family. House blew to smithereens. Nothing left but sticks and insulation. Two neighbors killed as well."

"Good Lord!" O'Neel reacted.

"How? Why?" Peter asked.

"The how's easy, the why not so much, but we can guess. Fire Chief Daniels says a gas leak. All of them, all four walked in after seeing a movie, one of those Batman flicks. That according to witnesses and a theater stub one of the uniforms found ...

"Someone switched on the light and wham! It blew. Daniels and his crew, my uniforms, the ones I could spare, and the coroner are still over there picking up the pieces, looking for any explosive residue, bagging the remains for sorting later."

*

Two days later the police department had returned to near normal. The ME had finished with the bodies from the Lansing blast, returned to their families for burial, or, in the case of the Lansings, who had no surviving family, to Gray's Funeral Home.

Chief Allen received a call from the medical examiner.

"You finished with Stark and Powers, Ben?"

'Ben' was Dr. Benjamin Sonnenfeld, whose various degrees and certificates of specialization read 'Stanford Medical School.'

"Yeah, we're getting them ready for you to-day."

"Well?"

"Oh, you want to know the cause of death, I suppose?"

"Yes, Ben. You are trying my patience. I've got these revolutionaries to stop, so, cause of death might help."

"Whenever I have the death of a young person with no visible cause, I run all the toxicology and drug protocols. If nothing shows, I turn to 'Michael Clayton.'"

"What ... who the hell is 'Michael Clayton'?"

"The film. They kill a guy by injecting him between his toes with potassium chloride. Stopped his heart in seconds. Most examiners would never look there. I saw the film and I looked. If you want someone dead and to make it look like an ordinary heart attack, that's your ticket."

"And?"

"Sure enough. Both bodies had tiny needle holes between their big toe and the second one. Then I ran the protocols for potassium chloride. Positive in both cases."

"Whew! But why bother disguising the cause? They were going into that compactor anyway."

"Best guess. Guarantee ... in case they didn't go in."

"Maybe the killer or killers just wanted them mangled ... or they saw 'Michael Clayton.'"

"Yeah. You should get the bodies later today, Mike."

"'Michael Clayton' ... Good film?"

"George Clooney. Recommended."

"Thanks, Ben."

*

After the deaths of Stark and Powers, Ayman Hamouda (who had now taken his mother's name) and Drew Hainey realized the law would hunt them down, but that didn't mean they had given up killing. They may have been sufficiently egotistical to imagine themselves clever enough to avoid capture. They were smart enough, however, to know that eventually someone, maybe even the cops, would discover their prison correspondence, some or all of it cataloged or read by prison authorities. (They had no illusions about their jailer's respect for civil liberties.)

If that happened, if the police got their hands on the correspondence, it would reveal the connection to their recruits, including Stark and Powers. Put another way, it would tie the Arco pair, who had shown no regard for human life, to the mayhem they had deliberately unleashed.

In a cruel twist, the Arco pair's 'by any means necessary' came to mean the 'necessity' of going underground with the expectation that their recruits would sacrifice themselves as human shields.

But would recruits do so? Wasn't loyalty a two-way street? Perhaps the founder's presumed defenders would balk at sacrificing themselves for men who had shown a cold-blooded willingness to forfeit the lives of others in the employ of their manifesto.

The posthumous message from Stark and Powers? Hainey and Hamouda, should watch their backs.

16

The blast at the Lansing home, now under investigation as a possible act of domestic terrorism, brought the FBI back into the picture. Special Agent Tom Wilson stood in Mike Allen's reception room, waiting to see the boss, rarely taking his eyes off the buxom receptionist.

Wilson's badge, contained in a leather folder that he flipped open and shut with a flick of the wrist and the wink of an eye, made the receptionist, Darlene Harrison, nervous. For all she could see in that wink of an eye, it could have been a toy badge, but she dared not challenge him. She also recognized his voice from phone calls.

Finally, Allen signaled over the intercom that he was ready for Wilson. Pleasantries over, Wilson came to the point. What he had to say was not surprising.

"Mike," Wilson's familiarity didn't sit well with Allen, "I'm afraid I'm gonna must step on your toes. This thing with the Lansings and other murders, possibly related, have moved the needle into the domestic terror basket. That's our jurisdiction ...

"I want to work *with* you on this but in the lead. I know you've put time in on the local stuff, so, why don't you brief me on where you are and have your receptionist gather up all the pertinent files."

Big Mike stared at a pissed-off Wilson. The Bureau had passed on the case earlier and now wanted to horn in—for the glory, Mike was sure.

'Take everything *we've* done and pretend they did it. That's how the f***ers worked!'

"Darlene," he said over the intercom, trying not to sound alarming or in a hurry. "Gather up all we have on the Lansing murders, including the house explosion, put it all in one of those embossed, monogrammed binders we just paid a fortune for, and bring it in here."

Wilson knew when the chief was playing him. He reached over Big Mike's desk, pushed the chief's hand aside and pressed the intercom himself.

"And don't forget the red ribbon, Darlene," he said sweetly.

Of course, this banter left poor Darlene thoroughly confused.

"Chief?"

"He was pullin' your leg, Darlene. Just throw it all in a paper bag and bring it in here."

Allen's instruction ended the jousting.

"What's the latest you got, Mike?"

More informality. Allen thought for a few moments before answering.

"Well," he finally decided to give Wilson something, "you wanna know how Stark and Powers died?"

"You mean two of the guys in that list of correspondence from Parnall?"

"Yep."

"Potassium chloride injections between their toes. You seen many of those?"

Big Mike knew the answer before Wilson could reply.

"No, but I've heard of it. Anything on who did that?"

"Nope."

What about Lansing senior and his wife, or the Lansing house explosion? Anything there?"

"Zip."

"Anything tying Robinson and Hainey to any of it."

"Nope."

"Jeez, Mike, what've you and your guys been doing up here?"

"Well, I'll tell you Special Agent Wilson, just waitin' for the FBI to finally be troubled enough to come waltzin' in here without so much as a 'Howdy-Do' and relieve me of my command."

"No need to get snippy, Chief. I got people givin' me orders, too."

"That's a damn shame, Tom. But let's not waste any more of your precious time. Why don't you go out there and wait for Darlene to finish packin' your bag."

Agent Wilson got up without a word or a look, strode out and closed the door behind him.

Darlene told the chief later that Wilson took his bag and left without speaking a word. Not even goodbye.

17

Chief Allen ordered his lead detectives to access the NI-BRS and milk it for everything about any 'one percent' murders statewide.

"I'm mindful of patterns—timing ... Let me emphasize the point. I *believe* in patterns. Those two guys issue a manifesto. Does anything nefarious happen after that? We need to know. If so, how soon? Does anyone openly justify their actions because of that screed? Again, we need answers to those questions."

"Here's a quick answer for you, Chief," Stan O'Neel said. "We haven't found anyone who refers to the manifesto, but there are plenty who justify anything that's done on behalf of an idea contained in it."

"Hmm, I'm thinking. Can we get our hands on one or two of those who, like you say, justify behavior on behalf of those half-baked ideas."

"Get our hands on, Chief? Not sure what you mean by that. I don't think we can go out and grab someone for what they say. We do have a 1st Amendment."

"No, no, of course we can't do that, Peter, but what if one or two such persons did things for which we could bring 'em in?"

"Let me see, Chief," O'Neel picked up the thread. "I'll get out our manual, you know the one, that explains how we can violate the 1st Amendment without violating the 1st Amendment. Don't you keep it on top of your desk, Chief?"

"Goddammit, Stan, this ain't funny!" Big Mike fumed. "Now you two get out of here and do your jobs. Bring me two of those idiots, *capeesh*?

*

Two days later, a Wednesday, the department's lead forensic investigator asked Darlene Harrison for an appointment with the chief.

Darlene's job was like that of a chief of staff. Manage the chief's activities and schedule or not schedule anyone who asked to see him. That included the department's lead forensic investigator.

"Not sure he can see you today, Fred. How 'bout next Tuesday after lunch, say 14:15."

"Jesus H. Christ, Darlene!" he screamed in the phone. "You've got to prioritize me, Darlene. MUST. I've got critical information about the Lansing explosion."

Now, Darlene knew the Lansing case was of great concern to Big Mike. He'd made that quite clear. Sometimes even a chief of staff must climb down.

"Oh, sorry, Fred. I'll put you through to him right away."

'Fred' was Frederick Anderson, trained by the FBI at their Quantico academy in criminal investigation and forensic analysis of crime scenes and evidence.

"Get up here pronto, Fred. Darlene will let you right in."

"What've you got, Fred? We're hurting for something."

"Well, first off you can now say the Lansing explosion was murder. It was no accident."

"How so?"

"Someone had disconnected the gas line to the water heater. Nothing related to a fire or explosion would explain that. Someone tampered with that line."

"Who?"

"Glad you asked. Very little fire occurred after the explosion, especially in the kitchen. The water heater was in a closet off the kitchen. The fire department responded quickly, so the water and lines attached to the heater weren't much damaged. That's how we know someone unscrewed the threaded attaching nut ..."

"Okay, Fred, but the 'who'? You were going to answer that, I thought."

"I am, sort of, but I thought you should know we got some latent prints from the line and the nut—even though the culprit would have needed a wrench to unscrew it."

"And your latents?"

"Sent 'em to the FBI lab. Just came back. That's why I wanted to see you right away."

"For God's sake, Fred, you sure know how to beat around the bush. So, you're here now and dammit I'm still waiting!"

"I first wanted to take you step by step through our process ..."

"Haven't you finished with that?"

"... of eliminating family members and every service person from the gas company ... William Richards."

"Huh?"

"That's your guy ... William Richards. Ring a bell? Should."

Allen had to sit back and try to process the name. Obviously, Anderson expected him to recognize it. His mind had turned into a Rolodex, with names flipping by rapidly, one after another.

"Disorderly conduct; assaulting a police officer; resisting arrest. That William Richards? The guy with the bull horn in front of city hall, handing out copies of that manifesto, stirring up the gathering crowd just before they broke in and started smashing anything they could get their hands on? That William Richards?"

"Bingo!"

"*He* tampered with the Lansing's gas line? He killed 'em?"

"The one and only. You gotta find this guy, Mike, before he kills again."

"How did he get access to the Lansing house?"

"Don't know. Maybe someone left it unlocked or had a way to unlock it?"

"Not likely for a guy fearing for his life. Maybe someone slipped him a key. Check with all the locksmiths in the county. Find out if any of them changed the locks on the Lansing house since his parent's murders. This one-percent conspiracy could have swept up all sorts of disgruntled people, sympathetic for one reason or another to an attack on the system."

"So, the guy who changed the locks, assuming someone did, kept a key and gave it to Richards?"

"Now you're thinkin' like a *real* cop, Fred. Better be careful."

Both men laughed, despite the unpleasant nature of their conversation.

18

Detectives Stan O'Neel and Peter Kenmar continued their investigation of the Lansing case, theorizing the explosion was not an accident. Barnhart Plumbing's William Richards emerged as the prime suspect. His fingerprints tied him to the water heater.

But how did he get into the house? Possibly it was perfectly innocent, a request for servicing. But why would he leave the gas line unattached? The Lansings would have smelled the gas immediately. So, the detectives dismissed that idea. That left them with the more likely premise that somehow, he got access to the home when no one was there. But who? Their list of suspects included David Lansing or a person or persons unknown.

Consider David Lansing. The explosion killed his entire family. A murder-suicide? Did he kill his wife because she was having an affair? Was she stealing from him? He didn't want to live after she was gone, so, he killed both? What about the children? What did he have against them? It didn't add up.

That left the detectives with murder. Someone wanted Lansing dead. Again, a person or persons unknown. Richards? Why would a plumber want to kill the Lansings? Did someone with a grudge hire him to open the gas line?

O'Neel checked his notes and confirmed Lansing's phone call with Kenmar who had listened in on a second phone.

"The guy called himself, 'Mr. Justice,'" Peter Kenmar recalled.

'Mr. Justice' had threatened the entire family. If Lansing didn't surrender his father's financial holdings, he'd kill his family one by one until he complied fully. So, the children were not collateral.

"Get on NI-BRS and see if anyone else reported an attempted or successful extortion by a 'Mr. Justice,'" O'Neel instructed Kenmar.

An hour passed.

"You're not going to believe this, Stan,' Kenmar told a seated O'Neel.

What he said caused O'Neel to snap forward in his chair and up to his feet.

"At least a half-dozen other instances statewide. All by someone calling himself, 'Mr. Justice.'"

"So, no murder-suicide, no botched job. This was an execution Mob style. Lansing didn't pay, as far as we know, and he went to the cops. All that wasted advice about using a burner phone. Whoever this was, is damn good!

"Look, we need to know whether Lansing paid up. Let's take this to the chief and ask for a probable cause warrant from Judge Holmes to access Lansing's bank account. I think we have enough to satisfy the ol' boy."

*

"Listen, Chief, we're still not sure who let the plumber into the Lansing place before the explosion. One possibility is David Lansing. One working theory is that Lansing set up the whole thing, possibly in a murder-suicide ..."

"Hold it right there, Stan. 'Murder-suicide'?

"Maybe the wife was having an affair, and he found out."

"Hmm, keep going."

"Maybe murder. He had insurmountable debts, and he wanted to kill only himself to hold off the creditors. So, he arranged the hit, but it went south and the whole family died unintentionally."

"So?"

"He told us he was being extorted by someone calling himself, 'Mr. Justice.' If he was being extorted, that eliminates him as a suspect. We want to know whether he withdrew a large sum from his bank account, money that had been his father's—that was the extortionist's demand. If he withdrew substantial amounts from the bank, he wouldn't pay off the extortionist *and* kill himself!"

"Then where are we?"

"We still don't know who let Richards—the plumber—in, so, we want you to get a probable cause warrant from Judge Holmes to check

Lansing's bank account for a large withdrawal or several large withdrawals."

"And where's the probable cause?"

"NI-BRS shows that the 'Mr. Justice' scheme played out statewide. At least a dozen other copy-cat extortions using that ploy!"

Big Mike drummed the fingers of his right hand on his desk, staring blankly at the two men in front of him. His detectives looked at their chief, then back and forth at each other, waiting for their answer.

Only seconds later, which seemed an eternity to O'Neel and Kenmar but was probably no more than a quarter of a minute, the chief stopped drumming and stood.

"Okay, write it up, and I'll take it to Holmes. When you've finished, find me the guy who let the plumber in! Let's wrap this thing up, pronto. *Capeesh*?"

But neither man heard the 'pronto-*Capeesh*' thing. Both had scrambled out the door when they heard 'Okay, write it up.'

19

Charles Butler's job at Security Masters didn't provide much income when measured against the economic clout of the one percent, but it put food on the table, and it kept his wife, Mabel, mostly satisfied. But Charles was an internet gambler, and he'd run up a huge debt.

What Charles failed to appreciate was the unfortunate truth that the size of his debt was no secret to internet hackers, always on the prowl to cash in on people of weak character and will power.

The size of the company where Butler worked and its shops throughout the Bay Area were like other sprawling plumbing and electrical firms that had succeeded in gobbling up the small fries. And, like those other giant firms, Security Masters maintained records of services provided to hundreds of clients, services that included installation of security systems and locks of all sorts on the gates and doors of businesses and households.

*

On a day inauspicious for many reasons, a man intercepted Charles Butler on his way to work, an event that would make that day auspicious. The locksmith was late and in a hurry. He'd just come from an unpleasant early morning spat with his wife over his habit of leaving his clothes strewn across the bedroom floor, a marker, too, of his movements throughout the home. Mabel was right to complain, of course, but for some perverse reason that invariably grabbed hold of him, instead of acknowledging he was wrong, he had to argue about it, an argument he couldn't possibly win due to the factual evidence.

"Charles Butler?"

The locksmith was sure he'd heard his name as he climbed out of his car in the Security Masters parking lot.

A man approached him without introducing himself.

"You have a minute, Mr. Butler?"

Charles stared at the man, unsure how to respond.

"Who are you?" he finally asked. That seemed the obvious thing to say. He didn't like the look of the man (tall, muscular, dark skin), and he wanted to get away from him as soon as possible.

"I'm from 'Win Big!'"

It didn't register at first, and then the stranger, seeing Butler's confusion, explained.

"I'm 'Bob Smith.' I work for 'Win Big' the internet gambling site. It seems you owe my company a considerable sum of money."

Butler's knees began to shake, and his legs weakened. He knew now why the man looked as he did (tall, muscular, dark). He wasn't there to award Butler a grand prize.

"You want to unburden yourself of that debt by honoring a small request, or do you want to come face to face with the consequence of continuing to hold out."

Butler had seen the 'Godfather' films, and so he understood the import of the simple phrase the Corleone family made famous, 'an offer you can't refuse.' He believed he'd just heard 'Smith' make such an 'offer.'

"Your wife ... What's her name? Oh, yeah ... Mabel. She know about your gambling? The money you racked up with my boss?"

"You leave my wife out of this!"

"Are you threatening us, Charlie? You think that's a good play?"

'Smith' had opened his jacket just far enough to show the corner of something leather. Butler assumed it was a shoulder holster.

"What's the request?"

"You ready to play ball?"

"Yeah. Do I have a choice?"

"No."

"Then what? I'm already late for work."

"Simple, really. I just want a key made to one of your client's homes."

"Which one?"

"The David Lansing residence."

The name rang a bell immediately. He'd just relocked the entire home. He became suspicious.

"The one up in the Hills (Oakland Hills)? Why that place?"

"Yeah, that one. Rich guy. You like rich guys? He pay you what the job was worth?"

Charles had heard of the one percent, and living in Oakland, California, he lived close enough to it to have a decent grasp of its ownership of the United States. That smallish grasp, however, was sufficient to render Butler pliable to the persuasions of someone who might approach him, claiming to want to bring down the super-rich, and offer him a great deal of money to do same ... Well, offer money in the sense of ...

"You wipe my debt if I do this?"

"All of it. No problem. Better we get your money than rich guys like Lansing."

"Bull! Who the hell is 'we'?"

"That's not important."

Charles Butler could see by the cut of the man's clothes that it was important. His entire manner, his speech, that he could walk up to a total stranger and propose he help break into someone's home, that he knew about Butler's gambling debt, that he was evasive when asked who 'we' was, all said it was important.

"You're all rich bastards, constantly sucking us little guys dry."

But his addiction had trapped him, which was the way of addiction. It took from a man the qualities manhood, so much in need and so prized.

So, the combination of Charles Butler's weakness and appetite was about to alter the destinies of half-dozen people he didn't know or have any reason to wish dead. He would provide the key, and the David Lansings and the man from Barnhart Plumbing, William Richards, would die, Mabel Butler would become a widow until she wasn't. And 'Bob Smith,' whose loyalty might have caused him to expect otherwise, would he, too, eventually join the long line of Arco expendables?

20

A location known only to three people.

Ayman Hamouda and Drew Hainey learned of the Lansing explosion days afterward. The information came to them through an outside contact, Brian Downing, a trusted go-between and the only person who knew where to find them.

Brian Downing of Xenia, Ohio. If one were to assess Brian during his high school days, he would not fit comfortably into the usual stereotypes.

At 6'4" he looked every bit the athlete, but Downing didn't play football or basketball. He chose not to use his physical stature as others of his size did, despite the difference he might have made on the basketball team. What he did do was study. Brian's commitment to learning made him something of a loner, as might be supposed, and he wasn't particularly interested in girls. Still, no one thought him a nerd.

After graduation, he shunned the major university in his own state, the Ohio State University. Despite having to pay out-of-state tuition, he chose instead the school most know as Ohio State's principal football rival, the University of Michigan.

Downing's usefulness to Hamouda and Hainey began there, in Ann Arbor—although he didn't know how useful at the time—when he chose to major in English and linguistics with a sub-major in applied linguistics.

*

Applied linguistics is a practical use of language that identifies, investigates and offers solutions to language-related, real-life problems. For those who want to go deep into the weeds, the major branches of applied linguistics pertinent to Downing's involvement with Hamouda and Hainey might include language assessment, forensic linguistics and translation.

*

Downing met Ayman Hamouda and Drew Hainey at The Halfass, a grimy burger, fries and beer joint where the three young men frequently hung out. They stayed in touch throughout their four years at U of M, exploring subjects together, many of them admittedly quite esoteric, subjects that held little interest for most students, and went separate ways thereafter.

When Hamouda and Hainey began to consider their response to the one percent and American policy in the Middle East, they remembered Downing and his major in linguistics. At the time, they were trying to figure out a communications system that would allow them to transmit indecipherable instructions to a statewide network of 'associates.'

They managed to locate Downing and engaged him in conversation over several months.

They came away convinced his economic and political views aligned with their own, and he was a person they could trust. One must also imagine that Downing's size represented a degree of physical security to the Arco duo that their average size didn't.

Xenia, Ohio, was by no stretch of imagination the Fiskhorns or Poletown Easts, and the Downing family was solidly middle class. But Brian did not need to have lived there to understand intellectually places like those and other inner cities in America's metropolises.

Hamouda and Hainey persuaded Downing, then an associate professor of linguistics at Miami of Ohio, to create a critically important, code that would meet Hamouda and Hainey's goals. The Arco duo would then communicate in Downing's 'language' via the postal system.

*

It was Downing who told the pair of the executions of Stark and Powers. Then he grew somber.

"What are you going to do about Brad Coleman and Nick Forrest, the hospital orderlies who took care of Stark and Powers?"

Before they could answer, Downing had another question.

"What about the guy from Barnhart Plumbing? The locksmith from Security Masters? I don't think you can or should trust either."

"Why in God's name would anyone suspect a locksmith's involvement?" Hainey asked the messenger.

"Listen, Drew," Downing, replied, "with all due respect, the cops are not dumb. It's within the realm of possibility, in my opinion, they might at least consider murder ... It would be a dereliction if they didn't. Next, they would ask *how* someone did it and could very well decide someone got into the house and arranged a gas leak. And how did they get into the house?" he said, staring at them, waiting for reason to take over. *"There's* your liability."

After a few seconds of silence, Downing had his answer.

Ayman seemed not to have heard Downing or understood how the locksmith was a liability.

"I don't think we can live with Coleman and Forrest," Hamouda said. "What assets do we have for that problem?"

A-round and a-round it went, and where it should or would stop no one could say.

*

Cover-ups were lies, which, in the hands of the Arco duo, evolved into more lies. A liar must keep lying to protect the first lie. A murderer must keep murdering to cover-up the first murder. You kill Robert and Emily Lansing. Then you kill the guys who killed the Lansings. Then you kill the guys who killed the guys who killed the Lansings, *ad infinitum*.

Next you kill Lansing's son because he went to the cops. Then you kill the guy who unscrewed the Lansing gas line that killed Lansing's son and his family. Then you must kill the locksmith who made a key for the guy who unscrewed the Lansing gas line. When will it be the turn of the guy who killed the locksmith? When will it be Brian Downing's turn? Will Ayman have to kill Drew? Or vice-versa?

Lying and covering up murders in the name of someone's idea of a greater 'good' was the work of megalomaniacs. A couple of angry, maniacal young men who couldn't get past their pasts choreographed the lying, murder and betrayal from secret locations. They had become obsessed with the idea that someone had to pay for all the world's ills—anyone but themselves, of course.

There had to be payback for all the Fiskhorns and Poletown Easts and venture capitalists. There had to be a one percent solution and a payback for the intractable problem of the Palestinians, for their very existence. But when a person or persons unknown had finished all *those* paybacks, who would remain?

21

In the world of Hamouda and Hainey loyalty moved in only one direction—up. The bodies were piling up, but each player in the Arco duo's scheme to undo the power of the one percent believed his value would spare him the fate of others. For their protection, they'd double down on their loyalty to the top of the chain.

The Arco duo used loyalty exclusively to advance their interests and never returned it. Every player, every link but two in the chain of the one-percent solution represented a threat and therefore a liability.

*

"Jeez, Mike," Judge Fred Holmes exploded, "you keep bringing me this stuff about a one-percent conspiracy, but I gotta tell ya, if I approve this one, I'm skating on thin ice and so are you!"

Big Mike Allen said nothing. He knew Fred Holmes well enough to know he wasn't through.

"You're tellin' me that a person or persons unknown is engineering a statewide vendetta against rich guys, and I'm supposed to salute that crazy idea. I don't think you know me very well, Mike."

"With all due respect, Judge, I understand you must look out for lawyers whose client's interests are put in jeopardy by the cops going through their bank accounts. But there aren't any clients! No survivors! Hence no lawyers!"

"Whoa there, Mike. Slow down. *Maybe* no lawyers. *Maybe*. Hey, wouldn't the world be better off without them? But I digress. Okay, without any heirs, those assets go to the state, and that's where we're still lookin' at the possibility of lawyers."

"How so?"

"Well, there's a word probably unfamiliar to you. 'Escheat.'"

"Never heard of it."

"The state takes the property if there are no lineal descendants or kindred and no one else has a right to it under its intestate laws ...

"The burden of proof rests on the state, which it can overcome by proving it was unable to find any heirs. Some states consider escheat laws a source of revenue ...

"Here's what I'm gonna do. I believe you have probable cause to suspect foul play, so, I'm signing the petition. But get your butt, or your detectives' butts, over to that bank. If you're lucky, the assets will still be there and you can resolve the extortion question before the state's lawyers come swoopin' down like vultures, I get disbarred and impeached, and you go up the river, so to speak."

*

O'Neel and Kenmar's visit to Lansing's Wells Fargo Bank with the warrant showed that Lansing had not withdrawn any large amount. They drew two conclusions: Lansing had not paid an extortionist, thereby putting him and his family at risk; and, because he made no payout, the extortionist had Lansing and his family murdered. Their killer or killers remained at large.

*

"Detective O'Neel?"

"This is Sergeant Bradley at the 2nd Precinct down in the City."

"What can I do for you, sergeant?"

"We have a notice here that you're looking for any foul play involving a plumber or a locksmith. You still interested?"

O'Neel was interested, but he didn't think the 2nd Precinct would have anything useful. He wanted to be polite.

"Sure, whaddya got, sarge?"

"We got what appears to be a Mob hit on a guy named Butler. He had a card in his pocket that says he worked for Security Masters."

O'Neel sat upright and signaled Kenmar who was taking a statement on another case.

"I'm interested. You say a Mob hit. How so?"

"Circular 9mm pattern around the heart, then double-tapped between the eyes. Uniforms that found him said the bullets blew most of his brains out the back of his head."

O'Neel winced.

"Any forensics? Prints? Ballistics? Fibers?"

He was in *his* element now, his comfort zone, not in Judge Holmes's with words like 'escheat.'

"We're workin' on all that."

"Where'd they find him?"

"In a dumpster, alley behind Broadway, near Stockton. The ME's goin' over him at the morgue."

"You gotta first name for Butler?"

"Charles. Charles Butler."

"Someone notify next of kin?"

"I think so. Spouse."

"Dammit, sergeant! I want to know if someone notified her! 'I think so' won't cut it."

"Who's this?" a new voice had come on the phone.

"Detective O'Neel, Sausalito PD."

"Listen, Detective O'Neel, this is Desk Sergeant Braxton, George Braxton. You got a beef with our personnel you bring it to me. As I understand it, my sergeant was making a courtesy call. No need for you to go ballistic on him. That's what I'm for. You work for Chief Allen, O'Neel?"

"Yes."

"Well, Big Mike and I bowl in the same league. We share. *Capeesh*?"

There it was again. A cop that used language like a mobster. No surprise Big Mike and George Braxton were pals.

"Yes," he replied meekly.

"Okay, that's more like it. Now, here's Bradley again."

"I apologize for goin' off on you, sergeant. I just need a little more information about Butler. Name and address? I need to talk to her."

Bradley gave him Mabel Butler's name and address. He seemed to have taken no pleasure in Braxton's intervention.

22

Stan O'Neel took the wrath of Big Mike in the only way he could. He stood, shoulders bent slightly stooped and kept his mouth shut except to utter, 'I'm sorry. I f***ed up,' at the appropriate moments.

"Goddammit, Stan, alright, then. Where the hell do we stand with this Butler guy?"

"We checked with his company, Security Masters, and sure enough they sent Butler over to the Lansing place a day *before* the explosion. Our working theory is that he changed the locks at Mr. Lansing's request—due to the threats against his family—and gave a key to the gas man, William Richards, whose latents we took off the gas line to the water heater and the knurled connecting nut."

"Butler and Richards were part of a conspiracy to kill Lansing?"

"Sure seems so."

"What else? All we have so far is a lot of conjecture."

"Butler's dead, Mob signature. Double tap."

"You mean Mob-*like* signature, right? We don't have a Mob any longer, right?" he winked. "Wait. What about the plumber, Richards?"

"Nothing yet."

"Maybe he tapped Butler ... Jeez, these anti-one-percent guys leave their messes all over the country for us to clean up. For once, Stan, let's try to clean *them* up."

*

O'Neel and Kenmar rang the Butler doorbell again ... and again. Nothing.

"Is it locked?"

"No!"

Kenmar pushed open the door and called out Ms. Butler's name.

No reply. So, they entered cautiously, weapons drawn and began a routine room-by-room clearing.

"Whew!" Stan exclaimed softly while retrieving his handkerchief and placing it over his nose and mouth with one hand. "That smell means only one thing."

Kenmar followed suit.

They found Mabel Butler in a kitchen chair, arms dangling at her sides, her head lolled back. Two taps between the eyes, brain tissue dripping onto the floor from the back of her head.

"Oh, s**t," Kenmar muttered. "Whoever is doing this is moving faster than us. We'd better get some protection for Richards, if it isn't already too late.

*

They called for ambulance and forensics, then began the hunt for William Richards, beginning at Barnhart Plumbing.

"How can I help you?" Barnhart's female clerk asked pleasantly when they introduced themselves.

Before either could answer, a man engaged in restocking shelves climbed down a ladder and ran toward the back of the office/warehouse.

"There he goes!" O'Neel shouted and drew his piece. Both men gave chase. The man threw open a door at the rear of the warehouse and ran toward a pickup truck.

"Stop! Police!" Kenmar yelled and took a knee in classic firing position.

From inside the truck, the runner opened fire with an automatic rifle. Two slugs tore into O'Neel who was still standing, each making a dull thud. The impact threw the detective backwards onto the parking lot asphalt.

The runner's concentration on O'Neel gave Kenmar time to draw a bead and open fire before the runner could wheel toward him, sending a full, ten-round clip from his .40 S&W service Glock 22 toward the man in the truck. Seconds later a limp body flowed onto the asphalt to a sitting position, propped against the frame at the bottom of the open door. His arms and hands had fallen to his sides and the AR-15 tumbled from his lap onto the parking lot.

By the time Kenmar checked on O'Neel, rose and approached the truck, a pool of blood encircled the victim's buttocks and flowed toward his feet. Two rounds had struck his head, which would make facial identification difficult.

The female clerk had run out of the building, her hand over her mouth.

"Call 911," Kenmar screamed.

She stood, frozen, her had still covering her mouth.

"Now! Tell them 'officer is down' and to send an ambulance. Do you understand?"

The woman seemed in a state of shock, both hands now covering her face and visibly shaking.

"Now! Get going!" Kenmar yelled again.

She turned and walked quickly back inside.

Kenmar checked the victim for a pulse and found none, then ran to O'Neel who was bloody but no longer bleeding. He checked his partner's carotid. His head fell and he began to sob. Neither officer had worn his vest.

*

The ambulance arrived along with Chief Allen. He found Peter Kenmar sitting next to his partner's body, sobbing. Big Mike hunched down and put an arm around Kenmar. There was nothing he could say or do except to offer comfort.

Once the paramedics had loaded O'Neel into the ambulance, Allen faced the awful reality of telling O'Neel's wife, Mary, that her husband had died while bravely bringing a fugitive to justice.

The female clerk said she believed the man was Richards, which forensics confirmed. In addition to the AR-15, police recovered a 9 mm handgun and silencer registered to the dead man. Subsequent ballistic tests confirmed its role in both Butler killings.

*

The Sausalito Police Department and other Marin County service departments, the fire department, parks and recreation department and so forth, held a public ceremony for Stan O'Neel. Fellow officers, uniformed and plainclothes, held him in the highest regard.

Representatives of those officers and other city departments marched behind the hearse carrying a flag-draped coffin. The cortege, its silence broken only by the precision of the marchers' resonant footfalls, passed solemnly by Mary O'Neel, flanked on one side by her three children and her mother and father, and on the other by Big Mike and Peter Kenmar.

Following the department's male choir *a cappella* rendition of 'The Battle Hymn of the

Republic' at the burial, Big Mike took the folded flag from the lead uniformed pall bearer and presented it to Mary 'on behalf of a grateful city and department.'

It was a tough day for everyone.

23

"Peter! It's Mom. We've been so worried ever since we heard about the shooting down there."

Ralph Kenmar had given up dairying a few years earlier. Arthritis and more. An 80-year-old man had no business carrying on with the hard work required of a dairy farmer. He sold the farm, and he and Jessie went into assisted living in Eureka.

"Hi, Mom! What's up? How's Dad?"

"What's up, indeed, young man!"

Jessie still talked to her son as though he were a child. Obviously, that was how she liked to remember him. She certainly didn't want to acknowledge his being nearly 30 and engaged in gunfights with criminals down in the big city. He didn't mind. He knew treating him like a child was her way of loving him, and he felt comforted.

"Would it kill you to write or call occasionally? ... Oops! Maybe I shouldn't have used that word."

He smiled and ignored her apology.

"Sorry, Mom. I promise to do better."

"Peter, your chief called to warn us that we might be reading or seeing something on TV about a gunfight with some bad people."

"I'm fine, Mom. You needn't worry."

He said it, knowing full well it would make no impression. She'd worry just because he lived far away.

Jessie Kenmar paused to think about what he'd just said. She'd worry less if ...

"Why can't you get *real* job, even music or art, find some nice girl and settle down?"

"You mean 'find a nice girl' to give you some grandkids."

"And what's wrong with that? You'll want to have them someday yourself."

"Okay, Mom. I get it. Now let me say hello to Dad. Love you"

Ralph Kenmar took the phone from his wife and waited until he thought she was far enough from the phone to hear what he wanted to say next.

"Chief Allen said you nailed 'im good, son. We're so sorry about your partner."

"Thanks, Dad. Stan was a good man. He saved my life. Drew the guy's fire. Say, how's senior living? Food good?"

"I'll say! They take real good care of us here. I'm not missing a barn full of cows, what they leave behind and those milking machines. When you comin' up for a visit?"

"Just as soon as I crack this case and round up all the bad guys. Promise."

"What's all the killin' about, anyway?"

"Bunch of folks got it in for the one percent. They don't like the gap in wealth between folks like us and the super-rich."

"Well, your Mom and I don't much like it either. But that's no reason to start murderin' people. Can't we just argue instead of killin' each other?"

Peter sensed the strong possibility of a circular argument.

"Appreciate the call, Dad. Let me say goodbye to Mom."

"Take care, son," Ralph said and handed the phone to his wife.

"Bye, Mom." Take good care of yourself and the ol' man, will you?"

"Oh, Peter ... find me that nice girl, won't you?"

"Promise, Mom. Love you, Bye for now."

Jessie put the phone down and turned to her husband.

"I heard what you said to him, Ralph Kenmar. Did you really have to mention killing people?"

Ralph put his arm around his wife.

"Jessie, listen to me!" he said firmly but softly. Our son is a grown man and he's got a a grownup job. It's what he wanted. He's not shootin' people all the time! Give him some time. Eventually, he'll settle down and find that nice girl you want for him. But he's got to do it in his own time. We can only pray we're still around when he does."

Jessie looked up at Ralph, smiled and nodded.

24

On Brian Downing's advice, Ayman and Drew no longer occupied the same space. Downing, their valued contact with the outer world, shuttled between the two. He managed to persuade them that the Lansing case had unleashed a disturbing level of scrutiny. They'd overplayed their hand.

Law enforcement, shaken by the series of execution-style killings, now took the threat to the one percent seriously and had ramped up its tactics in a far more aggressive posture than Hamouda and Hainey had anticipated or could tolerate.

Drew was still outraged that David Lansing had not paid the ransom for his family's lives. He appeared to have thought it his due. Downing tried to offer perspective, but it was wholly disingenuous.

"We didn't scare the money out of him, Drew, but our attempt to do so launched a chain of additional killings and now an intolerable level of police scrutiny."

Downing wasn't sure what Drew thought of those 'additional killings' (the Butlers) in which the go-between, Downing, was heavily involved. Heavily involved, indeed! It was Downing who ordered the hits, acting on the Arco duo's directive. Thus, Drew could not have been too concerned about the Butlers. Both men were apprehensive the 'additional killings' had galvanized law enforcement.

Brian Downing was sure of himself about the necessity of the Butlers, but he wondered yet dared not ask if Drew had gone squeamish about so many murders.

Downing decided he needed to check whether Ayman had changed. After all, it was Downing's hide in jeopardy. He provided the Arco duo with a level of protection. Had he acted precipitously? Would the Arco duo hang him out to dry? Those questions required quick answers.

"You have any messages for Ayman?" he asked Drew, testing his suspicion.

"Yes. Tell him I think we need to dial back on our aggressive approach, which will give us the opportunity to assess law enforcement's capabilities and, if necessary, calibrate our response."

Downing was now sure that Drew, at least, had gone soft. Had the One Percent Gang fallen prey to jealously, distrust and doubt? Were philosophical versus pragmatic contradictions tearing them apart?

*

"Well, well, well. To what do I owe this pleasure?"

Special Agent Wilson had just walked through Chief Allen's door, having skirted around Darlene without so much as a Howdy Do or 'is the boss in?'

"The Bureau has initiated an effort to find the people behind all this mayhem. We're looking at one percent agitation on college campuses during the past five years ...

"It's our judgment this movement originated as part of the standard political exuberance that seems to be a constant of college life these days. Some of it turns out not too serious, but some of it, because of the violence associated with objections to the one percent, we must take very seriously."

"Well, what can I do for you? I assume that's the reason for your dropping by. By the way, how'd you get past Darlene?"

"Trade secret, my friend."

"She'll spill after you've gone," he smirked.

"My condolences for your loss, Chief. I know Stan O'Neel was a very good cop."

"Thanks. Now, what can I do for you? I assume this is not a social call."

"Chief, since several murders have occurred in your jurisdiction, some of which we know were related to the one percent issue, the Lansings, for instance. We'd like you to look at the Bay Area campuses for the names of leaders. We'll be working the larger scene statewide."

"What! You're going to *spy* on college students and you want *us* to do the same? Nice. Did the Bureau learn nothing in the 1970s? My God, Tom!"

"Calm down, Mike. I'm not suggesting you take photos of people at rallies. These campus organizations register with the school, and the leaders include their names. That's all. Out in the open. Perfectly harmless and legal."

"But then you're going to spy on those leaders!"

"Not unless they say something or do something that reaches the level of a threat to peace. As you know, since the 1930s the Bureau has routinely monitored groups, militias, for example, that have given the government reason to believe they espouse violence or plan to engage in violence."

"I don't know, Tom. You make it sound sensible, but you and I both know these things can and do get out of control. Then heads roll."

"I don't want to put you in a situation you are uncomfortable with, Mike. So, as you consider my offer, lease keep that in mind."

"If I decide to take you up on your 'offer,' how do you plan to compensate my guys?"

"I'm authorized to reimburse you for time and a half. Look at it this way, Chief. The Bureau recognizes yours as being a first-rate police department. This opportunity is a recognition of that. It could open other doors for you and your guys, Mike."

"This whole idea of referring to 'spying' as looking at which campus organizations have listed with a college or university is like putting lipstick on a pig. And please don't assume we're itching to be FBI agents, Tom. Give your egos a rest. I'll get back to you on the 'offer.'"

"Don't take too long, Mike. This offer won't stand forever."

Big Mike threw his head back guffawed.

"Oh, right, and what's your other option? You can't bulls**t a bulls**ter, Tom. Like I said, I'll get back to you."

Five minutes after Wilson left, Mike buzzed Darlene on the intercom.

25

The FBI Field Office, San Francisco. Two days after Agent Wilson's visit to Sausalito. Special Agent in Charge (SAC) Alvin Nicholson met with Wilson and the office's principal counsel, Steven Birch. Nicholson briefed Birch on the purpose of Wilson's proposal to Chief Allen.

"I don't think he went for it, Alvin," Wilson began. "He raised the usual liberal objection to what he called 'spying' in the context of Director Hoover's days. I explained the history of our operation and its urgency relative to the threat from groups like the One Percent Gang. I mentioned militias specifically."

The room grew silent for 15 or 20 seconds, then Nicholson broke it.

"Either of you see that Spielberg film, *Munich*?"

Wilson and Birch nodded.

"I got to thinking about it the other day, and I wondered if we hadn't reached the point where we're just going to have to hunt down these guys and take 'em out."

"Are you f**kin' serious, Alvin?"

"Hear me out, and then we can talk about it ...

"The Israelis called it, 'Operation Wrath of God.' As you know from the film, it was a covert operation directed by Mossad to assassinate individuals they accused of involvement, planning and operation, in the 1972 Munich Olympics massacre. The targets were members of the Palestinian armed militant group, Black September, and operatives of the Palestine Liberation Organization (PLO) ...

"Israeli Prime Minister Golda Meir authorized it in the autumn of 1972, and she created a small group of government officials to formulate an Israeli response. Mossad took the principal role in directing the ensuing operation ...

"The committee concluded that, to deter future violent incidents against Israel, they needed to assassinate those who had supported or carried out the Munich massacre, and in dramatic fashion. It lasted over twenty years ..."

"Pressured by Israeli public opinion and top intelligence officials, Meir reluctantly authorized the beginning of the broad assassination campaign ...

"The committee's first task for Israeli intelligence was to draw up an assassination list of all those involved in Munich. That was done with the help of PLO operatives working for Mossad, and with information provided by friendly European intelligence agencies. Mossad was charged with locating the individuals and killing them ...

"Critical in the planning was the idea of plausible deniability, that it should be impossible to prove a direct connection between the assassinations and Israel. In addition, the aim was not so much revenge but to frighten them ...

"The Mossad team consisted of fifteen people divided into five squads: two trained killers..."

"Stop right there, Alvin!" Birch said firmly, rising to his feet. "There's no way in hell you're going to involve the Bureau in something like that. What the *hell* were you thinking?"

"Somebody's got to do something, Steve. If we don't, we're lookin' at anarchy," Wilson replied, backing his boss.

"Oh, bulls**t, Tom, and you, too, Alvin. Agreed, we've got a few murders, but that doesn't amount to anarchy, for Chrissakes."

"They haven't been ordinary killings, Steve," Alvin jumped back in. "It's Mob stuff. Threats, extortion and murder. Then, they cover their tracks by killing everyone involved in the first killing. And they don't stop with those directly involved. They go after whole families. You play ball, you pony up what we demand or we'll kill your whole family, your wife's family, your friends, everyone you work with, and so forth."

"I'm not disputing any of that, Alvin, but you simply can't involve the Bureau in something resembling Mossad 'wrath' or whatever the Israelis called it. Now, as far as I'm concerned, this meeting is over—it never happened—and I don't want or expect to hear a word more about it. Tell me you're clear on this, Alvin. Tom?"

"Clear," Alvin answered sheepishly.

"Clear," Tom agreed.

*

Birch left, but no sooner had he done so than Nicholson waved Tom Wilson back to his chair.

"Thoughts?"

The two men sat for a couple of minutes without speaking. Tom appeared to be scribbling something on a note pad.

"I have to agree with Steve about using the FBI in that way, but here's another idea, Alvin. Bear with me. I'm just wingin' it, thinkin' out loud. Jump in any time ...

"We approach one of these domestic militia groups to do what Mossad did. If that doesn't fly, we create our own 'Wrath of God' to come down on these motherf**kers like they wouldn't believe. We just need to crack one case, get ourselves a live patsy, and sweat him or her for intelligence that will show us their command structure, their tentacles and their weak points. Then we begin to take 'em out in a way that scares the s**t out of the others."

"I'm not sure about a militia or militia groups, Tom. Those types are a little too crazy and too short on accomplishment. They like to run around in the woods playing paint ball or put on their tactical gear and strut around state capitols with their ARs and a bunch of clips. Same kind of crazies that shoot up little kids in schools ...

"But what have those militias ever done? First time in a serious firefight and they'd scatter like frightened ducks ...

"I think it far more likely that we could recruit some former military, especially SEALS, Delta ops, Green Berets. Guys who know how to sweat someone, how to slip up behind a guy and slit his throat and then get on with the job. Like those guys that got Bin Laden. You see that film ... can't think of the title right now ..."

"*Zero Dark Thirty*."

"Yeah, that's it! You see how cool those guys were? Navy SEALS. Tossin' a football around, and then without hardly a word, they saddled up, swooped down and brought that SOB to justice ...

"Remember how President Bush always was sayin'—but never doin'—'bring him to justice,' like we we're gonna arrest Bin Laden and sit his a** down in a courtroom so a bunch of high-priced and overpaid defense lawyers could lie their a**es off about what a great guy he was, and how we got no proof, and how he's bein' railroaded, and all the appeals they're gonna file—all the way to the Supreme Court. S**t! Those are the kind of guys *we* need ... the SEALS, I mean, not the lawyers. No one needs their kind ...

“Don’t those guys have wives, kids? People who can tell em’ what jerks they are, what whores they are. What’s happened to this country, Tom?”

“Tell you what, my friend. Millions in lawyer fees shuts a lot of mouths.”

26

Ayman Hamouda's not-so-secret location. Brian Downing arrived after his meeting with Drew. He drove his pickup into an alley in Thermopolis, Wyoming, and stopped behind downtown buildings that included an old hotel.

He flashed his headlights, and a few seconds later he heard the sharp clang of metal as the fire escape ladder tumbled down. He locked his pickup door, pulled on the ladder to assure himself of its stability and capacity to bear his considerable weight and climbed up to the third floor. Ayman waited at the escape door.

Ayman had decided to stay out of sight as much as possible. He confined himself to his room, a kitchenette with a small refrigerator and microwave, feasting on TV dinners and other prepared meals from a grocery store a few blocks away. Whenever Brian showed up, he brought along a two-week supply of fresh vegetables.

"What did Drew say about the Lansing mess? Have we got anything left to clean up? Any loose ends? Anyone else wander away from the ranch, go off script?"

"He said we're damn lucky they killed Richards. Drew thinks they'd have sweated him until he talked."

"I agree, but it's too early to start killin' cops, if that's what Ayman has in mind as revenge. We haven't finished getting everything in place."

*

And where was Drew's 'place'? Shoshoni lay roughly 45–50 miles from Thermopolis, but Ayman dared not drive south to visit Drew there. That was Brian's job. However, if either—or all of them—should ever need a place to hide, the three men believed they had provided for that contingency.

Ayman and Brian had discovered an old school bus in a junkyard and hired a crew of three unmarried agricultural workers to get it running—just. Instead of picking lettuce, artichokes or grapes, the migrants dug a hole deep enough to hide the bus in a parking lot full of potholes, abandoned from the look of it, 40 miles from the nearest own. The Arco duo believed there was little chance anyone passing by on the highway would think anything amiss at the sight of a nine or ten-year-old Ford 150 rotting in the rugged terrain. Still, the migrants had to work at night with only dimmed flashlights to guide them. Once the principal hole was finished, the migrants drove the bus down a 30 degree ramp into place.

For access from the bus to the surface, the trio cut a hole in the roof for ventilation and a hatch wide enough for a ladder and a man. Inside, they created a pit toilet with separate ventilation to the surface and left a small amount of dehydrated food and three mattresses.

Finally, the workers filled in the entrance ramp behind the bus with spill from the principal chasm, then scattered the remainder. They covered the hatch with a quarter inch-thick stainless-steel plate, measuring approximately 4' x 4' and vovered it with soil and rocks to match the terrain. A person in the bus could climb up the ladder and dislodge the heavy plate with a large crowbar. Anyone walking or standing on top of that bus would be none the wiser.

The night the three migrants finished the project, two men, each armed with a silenced pistol, crept into their room in an abandoned motel and shot each man in the head as he slept. The two then carried the migrants' bodies one by one to a waiting pickup, which they drove to a nearby ravine and dumped them over the side into the rugged escarpments intended to hide them from sight forever.

Did that mean there were two more liabilities? If so, would eliminating those liabilities simply add one, two ... It was anyone's guess how many more.

*

Drew chose a completely different approach than his partner. Why hide at all? Who could possibly suspect a grocery store clerk in a remarkably poor town like Shoshoni? Who would bother? By choosing Shoshoni he'd outsmarted them all. That sort of cocksure hubris oozed out of every pore of Drew Hainey.

Whenever Downing visited either ring-leader, he faced a standard line of questioning and warning.

"Did you wash down your tires and brush out the tread? You know the drill. If they nab you and/or your truck, they can soil test what's in the tread and figure out where you'd been. They're not dumb," Drew reminded Downing, "and they have a lot of science in place to do that. FBI labs, being the most obvious. That would soon lead 'em here or to Ayman's place."

27

The one percent leaders had sensed law enforcement beginning to close in and looked for ways to hide themselves. In the meantime, two developments occurred in the Sausalito Police Department. Chief Mike Allen set aside his reluctance to assist the FBI and decided on two strategies. First, garner all available information on William Richards. Some might call what he proposed 'reverse engineering,' but it amounted to starting at Barnhart Plumbing and working back until some plausible reason for his murderous behavior emerged.

Where was he born and when? Where did he go to school? Level of education? Where did he live most recently? Any family? Who, if any, were his friends? Where had he been employed before Barnhart? Who hired him at Barnhart? What was his work record at Barnhart? How was he evaluated? What sort of employee was he? Where an from whom did he learn to kill people Mob-style?

The other development was Allen's grudging acceptance of Agent Wilson's request that Allen's department survey local college and university political organizations for the names of those whose opposition to the one percent was a matter of public record. Wilson had made that one-of-a-kind request of Allen's department because of the series of murders that began with the Lansings. Allen saw no other means of ferreting out the murderous bunch. Wilson assured Allen the Bureau had undertaken the same obligation statewide.

As he outlined a plan of action, Big Mike painstakingly instructed his detectives and investigators that there could be no possibility, no hint of undercover surveillance or of a counterintelligence operation on threat of immediate dismissal and forfeiture of pensions. They were to do nothing that would open the department and by inference the Bureau to the kind of scrutiny and criticism that nearly brought down the FBI and CIA in the 1970s.

Clearly, Agent Wilson had assumed a huge risk for the Bureau in soliciting the help of the Sausalito PD, but Washington had approved his plan, but there was intense heat coming from legislators whose districts had experienced the same sort of mayhem as northern California.

*

Det. Peter Kenmar began his investigation into the mysterious William Richards at the impound cage. There, officers carefully examined, tagged each item relative to hot and cold cases. They placed the smaller items in clear plastic bags. They overlooked nothing; the plastic bags contained evidence as small and fragmentary as clothing fibers and hair shafts.

As suspects went, Richards was relatively clean. But one item stood out: his pocket change. His coins included recently minted pennies. From those dates and the letter indicating which mint had issued the coin, Kenmar was able, with the help of collectors and the target mint, to determine with some confidence where and when a mint released the pennies publicly.

Kenmar was particularly interested in the where, which turned out to be Denver. The mint told the detective it had coined Richards's pennies during the previous six weeks. Furthermore, the mint assured Kenmar that the condition of the coins indicated they had passed through very few hands. Did that mean Richards had been in the vicinity of Denver sometime during the past six weeks? It was a stretch but not an impossibility.

Next, he returned to Barnhart Plumbing which was not easy for him so soon after his partner's death. He learned some but not a lot about Richards. He was born in Woodland, Washington, in 1993 and attended the elementary and high school there. He graduated high 18 years later.

He lived Petaluma and commuted to work by bus. On his job application he listed no family, nor did the personnel manager think him a person interested in having friends. Apparently, he apprenticed with a plumber in Petaluma and took a class at the Petaluma Campus of Santa Rosa Junior College. Richards didn't have friends that he personnel manager observed, but he did say Richards worked well with others. His supervisors at Barnhart had no complaints.

Then came a bombshell. Kenmar learned that Richards had taken his annual, two-week vacation one month before Kenmar killed him. Had he been in the Denver area when the mint released those pennies?

As the police had not impounded a car after Richards's death, Kenmar asked the personnel manager if he knew how Richards got about, how he got back and forth to work.

"He rented, as far as I know. I did see him a couple of times in the lot with different cars when he wasn't using the bus system."

"Do you know which rental agency he used?"

"No, I don't. Sorry."

Kenmar didn't give up. He drove across the Golden Gate Bridge to Beach Street, just off San Francisco's Embarcadero, a principal location for rental agencies, where he showed his badge and a photo of Richards a clerk at Barnhart had copied for him.

He struck out on Beach Street but realized Richards might have rented in Santa Rosa. He struck gold at Alamo, his third stop. William Richards had rented a mid-size Chevy, and his gas receipts showed he drove it to Thermopolis, Wyoming, and back during his two-week vacation.

Richards's trip to Wyoming puzzled Kenmar, but an investigative policeman always has a hunch about a case, and the hunch that preoccupied Kenmar after Beach Street told him Wyoming was a significant development.

'What is God's name was he doing in Thermopolis, Wyoming?' he wondered over and over. He assumed Richards was part of the One Percent Gang because of his role in the murders of the Lansing family. And, doubtless, like many Californians who took their state as a place with everything a person could possibly want, he had no idea what would attract someone to exhaust their precious two weeks of vacation in hollow Wyoming. Was it possible that Wyoming had something to do with the string of one percent murders that bedeviled his department? If so, what?

28

The Sausalito PD's second investigative task was Allen's grudging acceptance of Wilson's request that it survey local college and university organizations for the names of those whose opposition to the one percent was a matter the students themselves made public: they had signed petitions; made public speeches; handed out information flyers; campaigned for student government on an anti-one percent platform—and so forth.

Big Mike's part in the campaign proved fruitless, but the FBI had a more positive result statewide. The Bureau located some obvious campuses where the antis were prominent, private and public, most of them along the coast. But how was the Bureau to proceed once it had names—thousands of them?

Privately at first and then not so privately Big Mike Allen told Wilson that, based on what the agent told him of the statewide survey, the FBI would never be able to identify the ringleaders of the violent faction of the antis by pursuing that tactic. Indeed, he told Wilson, those people had undoubtedly gone underground. How prescient.

*

"Whaddya ya got, Peter? What's on your mind?" Mike Allen asked his chief detective after Kenmar asked to see him.

Kenmar related everything he'd learned about William Richards, and Big Mike listened attentively.

"Look, Peter, I can't explain Wyoming, but, basically, it appears we've got nothing tying Richards to the one-percent gang."

"Except the locksmith," Peter corrected him. "Shouldn't we work the Richards angle since he knocked off Butler and his wife? Have you given any thought to that? Maybe you have, but I sure haven't."

He'd left Big Mike behind. The police chief appeared to be in another world.

"Who's the locksmith? I've forgotten."

Kenmar's instinct told him Richards was closer to the head of the snake than Butler.

"Well, he and his wife are dead, and we know Richards was the killer."

"And who are they connected to in the anti-bunch?"

"What about Richards, Chief? He killed the Butlers, which tells me he was a step farther up the food chain than Butler."

Suddenly, Big Mike snapped out of his locksmith fog.

"Yeah, Richards. Sorry, Peter. I was somewhere else for a few moments. I think you should revisit the evidence locker and go through his stuff. We just need a decent *sniff* of somebody up the food ladder to get us out of this stalemated investigation. Anybody."

Kenmar did as Allen suggested, but he came up empty—with one exception. Something he'd overlooked before—an unattached key. It looked familiar, but he couldn't place it right away. It wasn't a door key; it was flat and had a number stamped on it. He studied and studied it, Finally, it came to him. It was to a safe deposit box.

'But there? Which bank? Another search like the one for the rental cars?'

'If I show it to a bank manager, he or she'd know to which bank it belonged. They should be able to do that shouldn't they? Brilliant!'

*

"You're going to need a warrant, Peter," Big Mike reminded him.

"Yes, of course, but I'll need you to sign off, Mike, or Judge Holmes will throw me out on my ear."

"You again?" Fred Holmes expressed his astonishment hours after Allen signed off on Peter's request. "What's your probable cause?" he asked pointedly after perusing the document.

Peter Kenmar took the jurist through all the steps that had led him to his petition.

"I can't give you a warrant without knowing where and especially *why* you'll stick it under some banker's nose, detective. May I make a suggestion?"

"Yes, of course, Judge."

"Rewrite your petition to simply ask whether Mr. Richards ... That's his name, correct?"

"Yes, William Richards."

"Just ask each bank whether Richards has a box with them. They may not be able to identify the key by itself. He killed two people and your partner, correct?"

"Yes."

"I'm satisfied that's sufficient probable cause to ask the question. When you find the right bank and they verify the key is to one of their boxes, then you can petition me to open it. I'll decide then whether you have additional probable cause."

Kenmar left encouraged; Holmes had sounded friendly. He quickly got Chief Allen to agree to sign off on a rewritten petition when he'd done as Judge Holmes suggested.

29

Bank of America, Wells Fargo, Chase Bank, USBank, First Republic Bank, Westamerica Bank, Northern Trust Bank ... Peter Kenmar was getting a workout but getting nowhere. At each location he asked to see the manager—sometimes a man, sometimes a woman—showed his badge and Judge Holmes's warrant. Every manager looked him up and down, wanted to see his badge 'one more time' and read and re-read the warrant.

"It says here you want to know if a Mr. William Richards, address unknown, rented one of our safe deposit boxes. That about right? And some judge says it's okay for you to ask me that?"

"Yes, that's right. The judge agreed there was probable cause of a crime to make that request of you."

"Oh, what crime?"

"I'm not at liberty to say. It's part of an ongoing police investigation."

Hours later, patience running thin and his feet sore from walking, he got the answer he was looking for.

"You see, we have everyone listed alphabetically, not by box numbers."

"That's great! It will make this go much quicker."

Peter began scanning the names under the watchful eye of Bank Manager Rebecca Elander of the Bank of Marin, flipping the pages until he got to those with names that began with 'R.' He followed the list with his forefinger, 'Redmond, Renninger, Ribbert, Rich' ... Bingo! 'Richards,' of which here were several. When he got to

'Richards, William D.,' he looked up at Rebecca and flashed a broad grin.

'William D. Richards' had rented Box 541. He recognized the number being the same as the one stamped on the key. "May I show you something? A key?"

"Why would you do that? Do I need to see that warrant again?"

"If you like."

"Is it one of our keys?"

She seemed less interested in the warrant, now, and more so in the mystery.

"You tell me."

"Alright, I suppose it's okay. I don't think the judge would have expected you to stop with the name if there's a crime involved."

'That's the spirit,' he thought.

He pulled the key out of his pocket. She glanced at it and said she was going to get her master key, the one that matches the customer's.

After a couple of minutes, she returned and examined both keys. They looked identical to his untrained eye.

"Yes, they match, but I can't allow you access to the box without a warrant that specifically says that's okay."

"I can get that and be back in a few hours."

"We close at 3. Just so you know. Banker's hours."

They both laughed and he left, trying his best to hide his excitement. By reputation, detectives, are supposed to be 'cool'—at least in film and popular culture.

Kemar arrived back at the Bank of Marin 20 minutes before closing. Bank manager Elander saw him come in a went out to greet him.

"What do you have for me now, Detective?" He got out the warrant and handed it to her.

"Judge Holmes said I can look in 541 now."

"You still have your key?"

"Yep."

"Okay, let's head for the vault."

Once there, they both inserted their keys, turned them, and Elaner pulled out the box.

"There's a booth over there, Detective. You can open it there."

He found the box empty except for a single envelope. He slit it open with his finger and shook out another key.

30

The entire contents of William Richards's box amounted to a key that looked very much like a key to another safe deposit box. But the key and stamped number did not resemble the one used to open the box at hand. He summoned Elander again, showed her the key and asked what she thought.

"It's from another bank, for certain. I can't say which one or where."

"Are there any experts who could help?"

"Wow, I don't know. Let me make a couple of calls. Do you have a cell phone with you? If so, take a photo of it in case I need to email it to someone."

The security officer for the Bank of Marin took Rebecca Elander's call.

"Hard to say without seeing the key, Rebecca."

"I can message or email you a photo."

"Message would get you a quicker opinion."

She turned to Det. Kenmar.

"Let me send him a message with the photo you took on your phone."

Ten minutes later the security officer had an answer.

"It looks very much like a USBank key. We have a catalogue with models from all local banks. That's my best judgment."

"Thanks, I'll let the detective know. Appreciate it."

"Hope it helps."

"USBank, Detective. He seemed reasonably sure."

He thanked the manager and left quickly. Five minutes later he was showing the warrant and the key to the bank manager at USBank, Philip Burns.

"Yes, it looks like one of ours. Do you know the box owner?"

"I'm hoping you can tell me that," Kenmar responded.

"I'll check our owner's list."

He returned with his master key.

"Well?" Kenmar said impatiently.

"Box 23 was purchased by a Philip Stark."

Burns's words stunned Kenmar.

"It's a delinquent account."

"Mr. Stark is deceased. Do you carry payment histories on box holders?"

"Yes, of course."

Burns excused himself to look at the payment file on his computer.

"Mr. Stark made the request for the box and made the first payment. After that, someone named Richards continued the payments ... until he didn't.

"When did Richards stop payments?"

"It became delinquent one year ago."

"Thanks. Now, I'd like to examine the contents."

"I'll need to see that warrant again."

When Kenmar opened the box, he faced yet another surprise. The box was empty, except for a road map of Wyoming.

Kenmar sat in the privacy booth off the vault, his head spinning.

'Richards traveled to Wyoming. Was Stark planning on a trip there as well? That couldn't be coincidental, could it? What's the attraction in Wyoming?'

Peter Kenmar had never been to the state. His only impression was of a place of vast nothingness, except for some interesting geologic topography. He also knew from elementary school and the encyclopedia his parents kept, hoping it would help with his schoolwork, that dinosaurs once roamed the state. There were bones!

At that moment it looked like dinosaurs and Wyoming were more of a sure thing than answers to the one percent murders. The more he thought about those huge beasts, picturing them as he remembered from the encyclopedia, the more he wanted to be in that place where they once ruled. A meteor may have extinguished them, but as things stood in the world, he wasn't sure that what came after one should think of as an evolutionary advancement.

31

Kenmar decided to have some fun, a diversion from the one percent case, and act on his years-old memories of studying dinosaurs and their bones.

His mind wandered briefly back to his happy days at school in the small town of Ferndale with Miss Harrison, Mrs. Mead and Miss Hanson. It reminded him again of something he'd believed for a long time. They were the most necessary and influential teachers, and the farther along the road of education one went, teachers and professors became less and less necessary and influential. It was the Miss Harrison's, the Mrs. Mead's and Miss Hanson's who made you who you were. He smiled and sniffed a little.

He decided to go down to the Sausalito public library, one of those Carnegie bequests, and pick up the story where he'd left it as a child. Childhood was on his mind. Nearly every kid studied dinosaurs; there was something mysterious and dangerous about those huge beasts. Their memory also connected him to something infinitely larger than himself. Larger in space and in time. They ruled so long ago. Space, size and time. He still couldn't wrap his head around any of it ... A good thing, he was sure.

*

What Peter Kenmar found in the library that day one could summarize as follows. Anthropologists believed the indigenous peoples of Wyoming likely knew about fossil evidence of dinosaurs 11,000 years earlier. A mammoth kill site of that age in the Big Horn Basin contained dinosaur stomach stones. Experts believed the Clovis people intended to use them as hammer stones.

Dinosaur fossils also inspired a Cheyenne myth about a kind of monster called an 'ahke.' The name derived from 'ahk,' the Cheyenne word for 'petrified.' Again, experts surmised the Cheyenne believed that mineralized bones found on the prairie or weathering out of stream banks were the remains of 'ahke.'

One of the earliest fossil hunting excursions into Wyoming happened in 1870, but the state's abundant dinosaur remains did not come to the attention of science broadly until 1877. A man named Wm. H. Reed noticed fossil limbs and vertebrae at Como Bluff after a hunt. Later, Reed and his partners uncovered several new species, including the first Jurassic *pterosaur* known in North America, and a new genus and species of herbivorous dinosaur. Not satisfied with that, they made another significant find, the first Jurassic mammal known in North America.

The excursion's finds continued. They included a new species of sauropod, *Brontosaurus excelsus*, that ended up mounted in the Yale Peabody Museum. And on it went. By 1918, Wyoming rocks had given up hundreds of tons of dinosaur bones.

Kenmar ended his research with the story of a Smithsonian expedition in 1940. Their biggest find and recovery was a nearly complete skeleton of *Uintatherium*. The specimen was exceptionally complete and highly preserved; the only missing parts were neck vertebrae, part of one forelimb and a hindlimb. Kenmar smiled when he read that to remove the remains, the team had to drive a truck up a dry creek bed and physically drag the remains out on canvas and pack them in shipping crates for Washington, D.C.

Peter Kenmar was in awe of these discoveries, but he knew he had to make sense of Wyoming in another context—the one he found challenging and for which he was paid and might be killed, like his partner—before more people, innocent and otherwise, were murdered.

32

The same day Peter Kenmar satisfied his curiosity about Wyoming's dinosaurs, Brian Downing met with Ayman Hamouda in Thermopolis. The initial conversation that ensued was the strangest ever between the two men.

"Did Richards leave anything behind that would tie him to us?" Ayman asked. He received a chilling reply.

"'Bob Smith' will wipe the slate clean."

It was the first time the two men used Smith's name in conversation.

"Give me simple, concrete answers, Brian. 'Wiping the slate clean' is too vague. If someone or something compromises 'Smith,' so are you, and if you're compromised, so is Drew and so am I. I don't think you want that to happen. Am I right?"

Downing had never seen Ayman so critical of his role. It meant he lacked confidence in him, perhaps even in himself. Either way, it should concern Downing. It was a troubling development.

Whatever pretense there had been for a contemporary Robin Hood approach to the one percent problem, Robin of Locksley had long since disappeared and replaced by mindless, mass murder, which, from all appearances, would continue until someone located and took out the leaders.

*

"Detective Kenmar? This is Rebecca Elander, manager at the Bank of Marin."

"Yes, of course. How are you?"

"I'm fine but I thought you should know that a man calling himself 'Smith' came in the day after you were here, also asking about William Richards's account. You think that's his real name?"

"What did 'Smith' look like?"

Even as he asked the question, he wondered why. He'd never seen 'Smith.' He settled for routine detective curiosity.

"Tall, Very tall and well built."

"I'm interested in how he knew William Richards and why he asked about him. What did you tell him?"

"Nothing. I simply said our customer accounts are private. I thought if I asked *why* he wanted to know, he'd get suspicious."

"I don't want to alarm you unnecessarily, Ms. Elander, but I'm going to take the precautionary step of assigning two plainclothes detectives for your protection."

"How will I know who they are ... or more importantly who they are not?"

"They will identify themselves in a safe setting."

*

"Chief, we need to talk."

"Oh, yeah? Whadaya got, Peter?"

"I've got what I think are three connected pieces of evidence, maybe crucial evidence, that I don't believe coincidence can explain ...

"First, a week before he died, Richards drove to Thermopolis, Wyoming, and back ...

"Second, the trail established by my examination of the safe deposit boxes ended with Philip Stark's box at the USBank. You will recall it was a key in Richards's box that led me there ...

"Finally, and this where coincidence really breaks down, Stark's box, which Richards paid for, contained an envelope. Inside was a roadmap of Wyoming ...

"Before I forget, a man calling himself 'Smith' showed up at Richards's bank the day after I was there. The manager told me he asked specifically about Richards. I think we need to assign two plainclothes detectives to the manager for her protection."

"Yeah, I can authorize that. But why would Philip Stark have a map of Wyoming in his safe deposit box? Does that mean Stark planned a trip to Wyoming? Like Richards's? What or who ties all this Wyoming stuff together?"

"Short answer?"

"Yes?"

"A person or persons unknown."

"But who ... Wait! Maybe not so unknown. Hear me out, then tell me I've got it all wrong ...

"We know that two guys calling themselves Robinson, or Hamouda and Hainey put out a declaration calling for the overthrow of the one percent ...

"We know that Stark and Powers killed a super-rich guy, Robert Lansing, and his wife, probably because someone thought they belonged to the one percent ...

"Some things we know; some things we don't. We know that someone murdered Stark and Powers. We know how but not who. Are you still checking with the morgue for any 'John or Jane Does' that have turned up recently? ...

"Yes, I am."

"We think Charles Butler, the locksmith at Security Masters, gave a key to William Richards, the plumber for Barnhart Plumbing who rigged the gas line at David Lansing's home after someone, 'Mr. Justice,' tried to extort Lansing senior's wealth ...

"We know that Richards killed the locksmith and his wife ...

"We know Richards made an unexplained but curious rip to Wyoming shortly before we wanted to question him, but he ended up dead instead ...

"We know that Richards's safe deposit box had a key to Philip Stark's box at a different bank ...

"And we know that Stark's box, paid for by Richards, contained a map of Wyoming ...

"Did Richards give the map to Stark?"

"Well, that's a darn good summary, boss, but we're still missing some pieces. We're back to the central question: why Wyoming?"

Allen continued his barnstorming rumination aloud.

"What could possibly influence to ordinary guys, presumably without a lot of extra cash, to travel to Wyoming? A money-making scheme of some sort? They were both part of the killer group taking out the one percent. So, did it have something to do with that objective? Were they ordered by someone to undertake that trip? If so, wouldn't a person or persons issuing orders like that be high up the food chain in the One Percent Gang?"

"I'm following your logic, Chief, and I'm going to complete your last thought and say, 'yes,' they drove to Wyoming to meet with Hamouda or Hainey or both!"

"What are you going to do about that, Peter?"

33

"There's another piece to this puzzle, Peter."

Chief Mike Allen and Peter Kenmar continued to speculate on the importance of Wyoming to their investigation of the One Percent Gang.

"I asked what you intend doing about that theory of yours, so, I want to give you some information that might help."

Kenmar was astonished. The chief's offer meant he was already a step ahead of him.

'He deliberately led me down that path,' he mused in admiration. 'Remind me never to underestimate Big Mike!'

"I know a place out there," Allen said with a half-smile on his face that exuded cockiness, the kind of confidence that someone has and knows the other doesn't.

Kenmar just wanted the chief to spill. He'd conceded to his cockiness already.

"I was curious when I first heard about it because it just didn't seem to fit my sense of Wyoming. So, I did some reading to sort it out, square it with my feel for its existence. It's miles and miles from any town ...

"I learned it was a very odd place. It's called, or people once called it, 'Hell's Half Acre.' I've never been there, but I've always been curious about a place of that name and its description."

"Explain, Chief."

"It's a large scarp about 40 miles west of Casper, Wyoming, on US 20/26. It was also known as 'The Devil's Kitchen,' 'The Pits of Hades' and 'The

Baby Grand Canyon,' all of those before the 'Hell's' appellation ...

"The 'Pits of Hades' seemed to me as close as anything to an accurate description after I did some reading about it. I understand you had a similar curiosity about dinosaurs ...

"It's a geologic oddity that encompasses a hell of a lot more than a half-acre—more like 300 acres—of deep ravines, steep slopes, caves, rock formations and hard-packed, eroded earth."

Kenmar was trying to take it all in while wondering when the chief would come to the point.

"I read that 'Hell's Half Acre' had an ancient and a modern history, the former probably more useful than the latter. Native Americans hunted bison at 'The Pits' by driving them to their deaths over the edge of the ravines ...

"As for the modern, a roadside restaurant, motel and campground that once sat atop the ravine are no more, and there is no public access to the cliff edge or the valley itself. All that remains of interest is vehicular access through a broken

gate to a large gravel lot (with potholes) from which the curious can get a closer view of the badlands-like topography."

"Goddammit, Chief, what are you suggesting about this 'Hell's Half Acre'?"

"Whoa here, Peter! Remember who you're talking to!"

Kenmar nodded and Chief Allen continued.

"Think about it, Peter. If you were a criminal and needed a place to hide, a place where no one would ever consider looking for you, would you consider a place like that?"

"Yeah, but where would you hide? You say the old motel and restaurant are gone and all that remains is a parking lot. So, where do you hide? In the ravines? How would you shelter yourself?"

"I'm going to sit here a few minutes more to give you time to think. I have an idea, but I'm not sure it's plausible."

Detective Peter Kenmar knew when someone was playing him, and he didn't like it. There was a crude way of putting the situation, and he rolled it over and over in his mind. The chief was f**kin' with him! He didn't believe he deserved it, but maybe the chief had a dim view of him, and this was his way of telling him. He opted to hold his tongue and take a diplomatic approach. But the chief had stung him, reduced his confidence rather than bolstering it ... Well, perhaps not to diplomatic.

"I'm going back to my desk, Chief. I can't think with you staring at me in a way that you know something I don't."

"I'll give you an hour, and then we can discuss it some more."

*

"Detective Kenmar?"

"Speaking."

"This is Doctor René Kincaid. I'm the coroner working the San Francisco morgue shift today. The orderlies said I should call you because you had asked about any unidentified 'John' or 'Jane Does' that may have been identified recently."

"Yes, thanks so much for calling, doctor. Do you have something?"

"Two 'John Does,' or they were 'John Does' until today. Some tourists spotted them washed up on Baker Beach. Decomposition made facial recognition impossible. I guess those folks from Tennessee, the ones who discovered the bodies, were pretty shook up ...

"Anyway, I checked with all the public agencies that would have fingerprints and/or DNA that they added to the Combined DNA Index

System. CODIS uses computer and DNA technologies to compare DNA profiles. Law enforcement, and I include coroners among them, of course, use CODIS to coordinate and share investigative leads. It took a while, but I got results that led me to the Santa Rosa Fire Department."

"And they knew your 'John Does'?"

"Yes."

"Who were they, doctor?"

"A 'Bradley Coleman' and a 'Nicholas Forrest.' The fire chief told me they were EMTs up there. Both missing for several days. It's hard to tell when they went into the water ... and there's something else you should know. Both men's hands and feet were bound with zip ties. In the case of the hands, behind their backs."

"So, they were murdered."

"Yes, and, as of now, the San Francisco PD is in charge of the case."

"Okay, doctor. I'll get in touch with them, tell them about our investigation and hope they agree to transfer the case over here. Thanks so much for our help. Really appreciate the heads up."

"No problem, detective. Good luck."

34

Detective Peter Kenmar couldn't wait to get back to the chief's office. More to the point, nothing could slow or stop him. He had news his boss didn't know and an answer to Allen's earlier evasiveness; the hour Allen gave him to come up with an answer about Wyoming had long since passed.

He dispensed with the required niceties in Darlene Harrison's office by ignoring them. By the time she reached toward the intercom to buzz her boss and before she could object, Kenmar had already breached his door.

"Jeez, Peter! What the ... Slow down. Take a seat and some deep breaths. Jeez ...

"Darlene!" he shouted through the open door.

She appeared at the threshold and threw her hands in the air.

"I couldn't stop him, Chief. Sorry."

He waved her off with his hand and a smile, as if to say 'no worries.' She retreated, closing the door behind her.

"You've got to call the San Francisco chief. They pulled two bodies out of the water at Baker Beach. Both murdered, both EMTs with the Santa Rosa FD based on dental records. Tell the chief you want jurisdiction because those guys are part of our investigation."

"How so?"

"Those EMTs would know how to inject someone between their toes and with what!"

"You mean Stark and Powers."

"I think we've got their killers."

Mike Allen studied his young detective, his hands together below his chin, index fingers pressed against his lips.

"It's a reach, Peter. Slow down. Think about it. Those EMTs might know how to inject someone between their toes, but how do you get from there to 'we've got Stark and Powers's killers'?" he said finally. "Not sure I can persuade the chief down there with guesswork. You can't tie these guys to Stark and Powers, can you?"

"No more than you can prove that Hamouda and Hainey are living in 'Hell's Half Acre'!"

"Touché, Peter, but not good thinking for a detective, especially one in *my* department!"

Peter, frustrated his boss couldn't see the truth in his supposition, took a big gamble. He'd throw Big Mike's logic back in his face and take the consequences.

"In all due respect, isn't that also the problem of your thinking, Chief?"

Kenmar watched as Big Mike's face grew redder and redder. He waited for the blow to come. But it didn't. Instead, the chief returned to the rational, raising Kenmar's respect for his boss.

"Look, if your theory holds any water, we need to find something to connect those four men. For example, how would those EMTs compromise Stark and Powers to the degree they'd have access to their toes ... silly as it sounds?"

Kenmar pondered the chief's question.

"I'm thinking! I'm thinking! ... They snuck up behind 'em and clubbed 'em over the head?"

Allen smiled in a distracted way that said he was thinking.

"What, if any, forensics do we have on Stark and Powers? ... Wait! How could I be so dense? I remember what the medical examiner, Dr. Sonnenfeld, concluded about the potassium chloride in their systems, but what was in their stomachs? Do we know?"

"A 'Mickey Finn'? Just wingin' it."

('Mickey Finn' was a Chicago bartender who preyed on drunken bar patrons. Finn or one of his employees, including 'house girls,' would slip chloral hydrate or 'emetic tartar' into the unsuspecting patron's drink. Finn's associates would then rob him and dump him in an alley.)

"But who would have given those guys a 'Mickey?'"

"'House girls?' ... Prostitutes!"

"Bingo! Let's go with that. Go over the toxic report on stomach content and blood, and if it turns up a 'Mickey,' find out if anyone's reported

'Jane Does' in recent weeks. Someone's runnin' a killing factory out there, and they wouldn't let any 'house girls' live any more than they let those poor bastards from Santa Rosa."

35

A motel at the western edge of Shoshoni, Wyoming, fifty-three miles west of 'Hell's Half Acre.'

What might a visitor think of Shoshoni, which took its name—with a slight deviation in spelling—from the Shoshone Indian tribe on the nearby Wind River Indian Reservation?

What would have attracted Drew Hainey there? The answer to both questions would likely be—*not much*.

Although established as a railroad and mining town, ranching had been the major agricultural endeavor in the area for decades but not exclusively.

A water-intensive mushroom processing plant began operation just after the turn of the 21st century. Staffed at first by minimum wage prisoners, troubled production led to the hiring of skilled labor from Guatemala, but some of those workers had immigration problems. Another problem proved vexing.

The plant's composting bunkers emitted unpleasant odors, eliciting numerous complaints from residents. The plant installed a stack and ventilating system to control and disperse odor from the composting bunkers, but to no avail. It went up for sale.

Other 'closed' signs abounded. Where there were sidewalks, mostly sand-blown, tree roots thrust the concrete upward and left it in broken slabs, reducing to zero the likelihood of anyone walking on them. Years of neglect and those roots allowed grass and weeds to grow from the cracks and between the slabs. If that weren't hazardous enough, untrimmed, overhanging tree branches forced anyone daring to use the sidewalks to duck. Streets were a much safer bet for pedestrians.

Generally, it appeared that whatever wasn't dead was dying. Shoshoni was a small town, which likely precluded money for upkeep.

*

Two men sat uncomfortably on metal kitchen chairs. A table to accompany the chairs, a bed that had supported too many overweight patrons and a TV set made up the remaining décor.

"There's no need to mention to Drew what I'm about to say. Understood?"

Brian Downing nodded his understanding, although he found it a bit puzzling. He settled for the 'need to know' formula common to all endeavors cloaked in secrecy.

"I want 'Smith' to take care of that bank manager at the Bank of Marin. But first, I want him to find out what was in Richards's safe deposit box. And I don't want a sloppy job that will require even more cleanup afterward. We've had far too much of that already. I want that bank manager gone in such a way it would be difficult to say she ever lived. Do you think 'Smith' is up to that?"

'Gone is such a way it would be difficult to say she ever lived'?

It seemed a tall order to Downing. Although he replied in the affirmative to Ayman's question, he was far less sure 'Smith' or anyone, for that matter, could make such a thing happen. He decided Hamouda's comment was figurative, not literal.

'Yes, that had to be it!'

He decided when he met with 'Smith,' he would present the instruction that way. As he packed to leave, he turned to Hamouda with a question, something that had been bothering him for months.

"Ayman?"

"Yes, Brian."

"You ever tire of killing? You may reach a point where no one's left. Is your feeling about the one percent worth all those people?"

Downing's questions clearly agitated Hamouda, so, he thought for a moment before answering.

"Because we've been friends and associates for so long, Brian, I'm going to ignore your impertinence."

There was a practical reason for him to do so: Brian's physical size in relation to his own.

Hamouda knew with a certainty beyond all other certainties he'd need to overlook Downing's impertinence for the right moment to address it.

36

Far enough from the light and the attention surrounding the jukebox, 'Bob Smith' occupied the darkest booth of the Rendezvous Inn, a bar notorious for showing blind eye to prostitution, bookies, narcotics and an occasional murder for hire, an atmosphere as seedy as any watering hole in the Bay Area's seediest locales.

Most Rendezvous customers, and there weren't many, sat on wobbly metal stools with cracked, faux-leather red cushions at a long bar doubtless sheltering a variety of weaponry. The bartender looked perfectly capable of handling all of it should anyone get too rowdy. Other customers occupied a half-dozen wooden booths like 'Smith's,' heavily defaced by customers' initials and scatology, and each equipped with a Rolodex of songs that played from the jukebox.

Oddly, considering its location in the super-sophisticated Bay Area, stuffed animal heads—deer, elk, moose, boar—cheap landscape art, western trappings and rusty ranch implements, the reason for which puzzled every customer who wasn't a westerner, adorned the walls.

A ceiling of dimpled, tinny square tiles coated with grease, many of them warped or partly detached, hung, it seemed, over everything. Galvanized buckets, apparently intended to catch the rain that seeped through those tiles, sat stacked in the dark corner near 'Smith's' booth. Dim table lamps seemed right at home in this atmosphere, as did the dust and grease-encrusted fluorescent fixtures that dangled ominously from above by jury-rigged wiring.

*

'Bob Smith' was a large, youthful-looking man with a craggy face that had seen too much sun. The purpose of the crags seemed to be to shield steel blue eyes that rivaled those of Paul Newman. 'Smith' possessed a full complement of coal black hair with no hint of gray around the temples.

'Bob Smith' sat with two men who, for lack of precision when it came to their names, passed as 'Frank' and 'Joe.' That was how everyone knew them and knew better than to press the matter further.

For the record and from a safe distance, 'Smith's' hires for his dirty work were Billy Roy Stewart and Junior Phillips, Jr. Junior's dad had insisted on naming his son after himself, and he had seen somewhere that sons named for their fathers appeared in formal documents as 'II' or 'Jr.' Phillips senior didn't think 'II' or 'Two' would work as a name, so his son became 'JR' or 'Junior' or Junior Phillips, Jr.

The size and build of both men, which lost nothing in comparison to 'Smith,' said loud enough for anyone paying attention—muscle men. The bulging deltoid and pectoral muscles of the two imports were obvious, as were other bulges under half-open jackets that deliberately said they were packin' heat. One should assume they had other weapons within reach.

'Smith' carefully explained he had two jobs for which he'd enticed them away from their usual 'employment' in Reno or Las Vegas. They were to make Rebecca Elander go away, and they were to protect 'Smith' from a fate he fully anticipated based on experience, yet one he respected. 'Smith's was a world alien to most but one he had inhabited long enough to feel comfortable with some risk but not all risk.

Billy Roy and Junior, both in their mid-thirties, had drifted out of the South and found a home with the Mob in Nevada. One should not assume, however, that the 'Mob' referred exclusively to the classic Sicilian brand familiarized in pop culture by Mario Puzo and the Godfather films.

Neither man had finished their formal education; both had left school at age 16. Their intelligence, discounted at one's peril, belonged to the category of 'street smarts.' They spent hours in the gym bulking up—their jobs required bulk—which doubtless led some to think of them as men someone could talk into carrying out assignments that threatened their wellbeing.

*

"Look, 'Mr. Smith,' if that's your real name," Junior began, "you are asking too much in the case of Ms. Elander. We *can* erase her but we *can't* erase her. You follow?"

"Yeah, 'Smith,'" Billy Roy chimed in, "what's all this bull**t about 'making her go away as though she never existed'? Who's asking for that? Must be outta their mind."

"Those were my orders."

"Well, 'Smith,' they're *not* ours. So, pay us the back half of what you owe, and we'll be on our way."

"The deal was, guys, you'd get paid *in full* when you finished the job. Not before! That's how contracts work. Elander, then you get paid."

"That your final position, 'Smith'?" Billy Roy asked.

'Smith' made a sudden move to get up, but Junior Phillips sat him back down with a shove. He realized he was in trouble.

'Bob Smith' knew he had to think of something very quickly or he was a dead man.

The three grew silent for a moment or two, exchanging distrustful looks.

"You're stickin' to that?" Junior said. "No money until we finish the job? We told you we ain't doin' Elander."

'Smith' knew he was in trouble, but he decided the best course was to sound tough—to bluff his way out.

"I'm stickin'—to use your word, Junior—as sure as anything." He sneered at the word 'stickin,' almost spat it out in obvious derision. "So, gentlemen, I suggest you get up and get out of here. Don't contact me again until Elander's done. *Capeesh*?"

Billy Roy and Junior looked at each other, then at 'Smith.' They may not have known the meaning of 'derision,' but they sure as hell knew what a look of 'derision' meant when they saw it.

"You got our money on you?"

"Do you think ..."

Before he could finish his sentence, 'Smith' felt a stab of ice-cold steel go into and then slice across his abdomen. He reached toward his supposed antagonists with one hand, which Billy Roy brushed aside, and with the other under the tabletop to find the cause and stop the pain.

But he couldn't hold back his intestines. Along with copious amounts of blood from his severed aorta, 'Smith's' slimy digestive tract slithered onto the floor toward the jukebox. A prostitute giving a hand job to a fat patron up against the juke, slipped on 'Smith's' gore, looked down and screamed. Of course, Billy Roy and Junior had long since skedaddled out a back door into the alley and their waiting car.

All of Brian Downing's education in applied linguistics meant nothing when measured against a sharp knife wielded by a man who had nothing close to his erudition and cared nothing for it.

*

A week later ...

"Peter, did you get the fingerprint results on the guy who was gutted at the Rendezvous?"

"Yeah, just got a FAX this morning. FBI lab ID him as a 'Brian Downing.' No record. Big guy. Well over six feet. Whoever did him must've found a way to distract him. Once lived in Michigan ... Ann Arbor. No next of kin. Address was an empty PO box in Petaluma."

"Anything more?"

"Well, you're not going to believe this, Chief. Two things. One, his glove box was full of credit-card slips for gas."

"And?"

"This guy was a regular traveler between here and ... drumroll, please ..."

"Wyoming!"

"Bingo. He last gassed up there at a town called Shoshoni, which is about 60 miles from ... drumroll, please ..."

"'Hell's Half Acre'! Holy s**t! Okay, I'm pretty sure that place is involved. So, get a sample of dirt or dust from his car. Get in touch with law enforcement in Shoshoni or Casper, probably the latter, and ask them to send us a sample from that parking lot. We can have the FBI Field Office in the City test both. He had to have picked up dust or dirt traceable to 'Hell's Half Acre.'"

"Chief?"

"Yeah, what?"

"You didn't ask me about the second thing."

"Forgot. Sorry. Is it important?"

"The gutted guy who once lived in Ann Arbor?"

"Goddammit, Peter! Out with it!"

"He's on the list of those who communicated with Hamouda and Hainey while they were in Parnall."

"H-o-l-y s**t! That probably means the person or persons unknown who gutted him are probably involved with the One Percent Gang. Did anyone interview the people who work at the Rendezvous?"

"Not yet."

"Then get you a** over there and do it!"

Two hours later the Rendezvous bartender had finished describing two men to Peter. They stood out from other customers, he said, because all three men in that booth were unusually muscular.

Peter had no way of knowing when he left the Rendezvous that the bartender had described two men who fit the physical profiles of 'Frank' and 'Joe.'

37

During a mandated, routine public health check of prostitutes who prowled the City's Tenderloin, police swept up Shirley Thomas and Linda Harris along with other 'solicitors'; both Thomas and Harris tested positive for a nasty STD.

As Shirley and Linda had reached the arrest limit allowed by health standards in the City, once the hospital had cleaned them up, each faced jail time, which they and their pimps couldn't afford. They pleaded with the nurse to falsify their records, but she refused and reported the incident to the precinct desk sergeant.

*

"I want a lawyer, goddammit! I got something to tell, and I want my rights."

"Not so fast, Linda," the sergeant responded gently. "First you gotta give me some idea what you think you know."

"I know about two murders, you jackass! Is that enough for you? I know who got done, and I know who dunnit."

"I'll see what I can do, Linda. Where do you say these murders happened?"

"Santa Rosa. This guy paid us to go up there and get a couple of guys drunk. I'm pretty sure they told us they were EMTs."

"You mean drugged."

"Have it your way, yeah."

"The matron's gonna return you to your cell while I see what's what."

"Well, I ain't talkin anymore without my lawyer!"

"I'm sure they'll get you a PD."

"That's more like it."

*

The precinct captain called the police chief in Santa Rosa, who told him the murders of two EMTs, if that's who they were, might be part of an ongoing investigation in Sausalito. That warranted another phone call.

"Chief Allen?"

"Yes."

"This is George Dunn. I'm the precinct captain down at the Tenderloin Station on Eddy St. We've got two hookers, one of whom claims to have information about two EMT murders. She says she knows who did it. She's lookin' at jail time she can't afford and wants a PD, which we'll arrange. We believe what she's alleging may be germane to your EMT investigation."

"I'd need to know more, before I could say."

"She's clammed up until we get her a lawyer. So far, we haven't sat her down with him or her. The case landed here because she did claim the two dead guys were EMTs from our fire department. They were."

"What can you do for me?" Allen asked.

"Send someone down to sit in on our interview with this gal and her attorney."

"I'm sending Peter Kenmar, our lead detective. Let me know when you're ready.

*

An investigator with the Tenderloin Station began the interview. The others in the room were Captain Dunn, Harris's public defender and Peter Kenmar.

"Have a seat Ms. Harris."

Linda wasn't used to being addressed so formally ... or politely. When she saw Kenmar, she blew.

"Who the f**k are *you*?" she blurted out in surprise and intended disrespect. "What the hell's goin on here?"

Kenmar ignored her.

Her rap sheet listed her age as 34. That was useful. Kenmar had little confidence in a hooker's age from their looks alone. The orange jumpsuit obscured whatever Harris's figure might have been. She wore her dyed blonde hair in a ponytail—Kenmar suspected that was only while in jail—and her face in a perpetual scowl. When she spoke, Kenmar noticed the missing, yellowed or blackened teeth. A prostitute and meth user, a not uncommon combination.

"What's a pretty college boy like you doin' in this hole?" she addressed Kenmar again.

As she spoke, she waved her arms wildly in a gesture that indicated the 'hole' was the lockup and interrogation room.

Because Harris kept speaking only to Kenmar, the investigator decided to let their exchange play out. If they reached a point that required intervention, he'd step in.

"My name's Kenmar. I'm a detective with the Sausalito PD. You *will* want to talk to me. I understand you think you have information that would interest me about a couple of murders."

"Maybe. If I do, what's in it for me?"

"Try me, then maybe I'll think about it."

Harris stared at Kenmar ... fidgeted with her handcuffs. Her PD sat silently.

"You told someone at the Tenderloin Station that you witnessed a double murder and that you knew who had done it. That correct?"

She stopped fidgeting and snapped forward in her chair.

"Damn straight."

Kenmar looked at the PD. He knew his next line of questioning might breach his tolerance.

"Tell me briefly what happened."

"That gonna spring me?"

"Maybe. It depends on how truthful you are."

"You never lie? Anybody ever threaten you if you ratted on 'em?"

"Just tell me what happened. If you're lying, I'll know it."

"Bulls**t! How?"

"Trade secret. I'm waiting, Ms. Harris, and my patience is growing thinner by the minute."

"A guy, a really big guy, said if we took a couple of 'Johns' up to a certain hotel room and slipped 'em some pills he showed us, we'd be handsomely rewarded. So, we did it."

There it was again, Kenmar realized. Reference to a 'big guy.' Was Harris talking about Brian Downing?

"Then what happened?"

"Saw two other guys go into the room. Pretty soon them and the big guy dragged out the two bozos."

"The guys who dragged out the two bozos, as you called them, those are the two guys who washed up on the beach."

"Yeah, I guess."

"Where were you when you saw this?"

"Walkin' down the street as fast as we could, but we looked back and saw them pile those guys into a car."

"Do you think you could identify the dead guys from some photos I have?"

"Damn straight."

"And what do you want if your information proves useful?"

"I want the f**k out of here, for me *and* my friend."

Precinct Captain Dunn guffawed.

"I can't promise you anything. You're not doing anything special. You're just doing what any responsible citizen should."

"Humph," she muttered and then spoke clearly and loudly. "Then let me out of here."

"You'll have to look at the pictures first."

"You think I lied?"

"No, I believe your story ... up to a point."

Kenmar rose, followed by Dunn, and walked to the door of the interview room and opened it.

"Where you goin,' man?"

Kenmar didn't reply. He strode down the hall to Dunn's office.

"Captain, can you arrange a photo lineup for Harris? I want to try something unusual."

"Unusual?"

"Unusual for a lineup. I think you'll agree. Get me photos of a half dozen of *your* guys—no uniforms—with a reasonable resemblance to those two EMTs. Tell her she's to identify the two guys from the beach. If she picks one or two of your guys, we'll know she's full of it. But if not ..."

"Then she's credible?"

"I hope."

*

Two hours later: Linda Harris looked over the photos of Dunn's men. Finally satisfied but wearing a puzzled look, she turned toward and Dunn and Kenmar.

"What the f**k you pullin'?" she shouted. "Ain't none of those guys the ones I saw. You take me for a fool or sumpin'?"

Kenmar looked at Dunn and smiled.

"Thank you, Ms. Harris. I have one more photo for you to examine."

"*Then* do we get out of here?" she said to Dunn.

"Do you recognize this man?" Department technicians had cleaned up the picture with Adobe's PhotoShop application.

Linda Harris took one look at the photo of Brian Downing (a.k.a. 'Bob Smith') and began to shake uncontrollably.

"Matron!" Dunn shouted toward the closed door. A woman opened the door and started in when Dunn asked her to get a blanket for Harris. When the woman's shaking had eased, Kenmar addressed her gently.

"Why did you start shaking when you saw that photograph?"

"You'd shake, too, if you'd seen that guy do what I seen 'im do."

"What exactly did you see him do?"

Harris had suddenly become vague about what she saw. Detective Kenmar could conclude she only saw a 'big guy' and the two EMTs drag Stark and Powers out of their hotel.

"Listen! I thought you cops were supposed to be so smart. He's the big guy I was tellin you about, the one who had those guys killed and then done somethin' with the bodies!"

"So, you don't know what happened to the two men who were dragged out of that hotel."

"I told you already I don't know nothin' about that."

Did you see the 'big guy' kill the two men who helped him drag those bodies out of the hotel?"

"I didn't see anyone killed. Never said I did."

"But you recognize the pictures of the two men who did the dragging."

"Goddammit, how many times do I have to say it? I done what you asked, and now I want out of here!"

The investigator looked at the PD and signaled he had finished with Harris and she was free to go.

As the room emptied, Kenmar turned to Dunn.

"Thank the 'lady' for me," Kenmar said as he brushed past Dunn on his way to his car in the police parking lot.

Peter Kenmar had mixed feelings about the interview. He believed Harris's account because she passed his lineup and didn't try to stretch her story beyond what she could confirm. He was confident the 'big guy' was Brian Downing, and he had confirmation about the dead EMTs. But he had no proof that Downing killed the EMTs. Glass slightly more than half full.

38

Tom Wilson had waited long enough, and Director Christopher Wray agreed. He lit a fire under Wilson with several specific inquires and subsequent directives. The San Francisco SAC had given Mike Allen plenty of room to move on the One Percent Gang, but time and Allen's silence told Wilson Big Mike was holding out.

Had Wilson's arrangement with Allen betrayed the Bureau and jeopardized his career? Quite possibly. Allen had not kept his end of the bargain to share all the details of his investigation with the Bureau. Wilson knew and Chief Allen knew it was supposed to work only one way. Credit for the win would go to the Bureau, not some unknown West Coast police officer.

If Allen was about to make an arrest or arrests, perhaps even hold a presser to announce he had cracked the case, Wilson knew, quite possibly at the expense of his career, he had waited far too long to shorten Allen's leash or cut him loose entirely.

He had tossed and turned in bed for several nights, even experiencing a nightmare in which the Director stood behind the blade of a guillotine before it plunged toward Wilson's neck. Why had he made the arrangement with Allen in the first place. Did it have something to do with his prior career?

*

Thomas Wilson came from a devout Catholic family. His mother, a widow by the time

Thomas was ready for college, attended mass every day of the week. Influenced, as one could easily imagine, by his mother's profound piety, it had been his ambition after graduation from Loyola Marymount in Los Angeles to enter a seminary and eventually join the priesthood.

But the Vietnam War put that plan, as it did those of so many others, on hold. The priesthood had always been his mother Mary's ambition more than his. So, rather than becoming Father Thomas Wilson (Fr. Tom), he would soon assume another title: Lieutenant Junior Grade Tom Wilson.

*

He had always wanted to fly, and his deep sense of patriotism led him to the Navy's flight training program at Pensacola, Florida. Tom Wilson had chosen to do something he had always wanted to do, something impulsive, and the war gave him the excuse to indulge that dream. What his mother thought would not be difficult to imagine.

Two years later Tom Wilson found himself in the seat of a F8 Crusader fighter jet aboard the USS *Enterprise*, a giant, nuclear aircraft carrier—the Navy's first. When required to deploy in support of the U.S. war against North Vietnam, the

Enterprise operated at 'Yankee Station' in the South China Sea's Tonkin Gulf.

Four years, several decorations and moments of stark terror later, Wilson faced a crossroad. He loved the Navy and hadn't lost his feeling of patriotism, although he believed some in his country had. But the anti-war crusade, which had morphed in some quarters into revolutionary violence, pushed Tom Wilson toward a new career: law enforcement. He applied to join the FBI.

*

"Chief Allen, I need a complete accounting of your progress to date on the one percent murder investigation."

Wilson's formal reference to 'Chief Allen' rather than 'Mike' or 'Big Mike' signaled his impatience with the Sausalito PD and the reestablishment of FBI cognizance and authority. He realized he should have done both after the Lansing murders. It chagrined him to realize he'd been lazy in asking a city police department to do his job. He couldn't explain it. The Navy would have called it what it was—a dereliction of duty.

"You want me to get Darlene in here to take notes for you, Tom?"

"No, thanks, I'll take my own."

“Okay, then. Begin with Stark and Powers. We believe they did the Lansing seniors. They communicated with Hamouda and Hainey while at Parnall.”

“What’s ‘Parnall’?”

“Michigan prison. Should I continue?”

Allen got a withering look from Wilson that told him he damn well better get on with it.

“Two prostitutes and two Santa Rosa EMTs did Stark and Powers ...

“A person or persons unknown did the two EMTs. One of the prostitutes ID’d the guy disposed of the EMT’s bodies. Called himself ‘Bob Smith’ but we’re sure he was Brian Downing, an associate of Hamouda and Hainey at the University of Michigan. Someone gutted him at a local bar ...

“Then we have Lansing junior. A locksmith, Charles Butler, hired by Lansing after he received the demand for his parents’ money and death threats against his family, gave a key to a plumber, William Richards, who unscrewed the gas line to the water heater, the proximate cause of the explosion that killed the entire Lansing family ...

“Richards then killed Butler and his wife, and one of my detectives killed Richards after he killed one of my detectives.”

“My God, Chief! ... That’s everything?”

"You're up to date, Tom."

"That would be 'Agent Wilson' Chief. What about Hamouda and Hainey? Where are they?"

Wilson's abrupt new tone puzzled Big Mike. He resented the sudden impersonalization of their relationship, but he had no inkling of the pressure Washington had brought down on the man across from him.

"We don't have a clue, Special Agent Wilson," Allen lied. He wasn't nearly ready to tell Wilson about Wyoming. He wanted that final glory to go to his guys after they wrapped up the case out there.

Wilson had stopped taking notes and looked up, staring blankly at Big Mike. Finally, he spoke.

"Good work, Chief Allen. We'll take it from here."

Allen wondered how that would be possible without his knowing about Wyoming. To stay a step or two ahead of the feds, detective Kenmar would have to press hard.

"What a clusterf**k," Wilson muttered as he rose to leave.

"Were you referring to the killers or my investigation, Special Agent."

"Wilson. Special Agent Wilson. I was speaking of a world gone mad."

39

Big Mike Allen met with Peter Kenmar and Cameron Beatty, Stan O'Neel's replacement, a youngish man Allen had promoted out of necessity from the uniformed ranks.

Beatty had an AA degree in public safety from the College of Marin, a plus so far as Allen was concerned. On the other hand, he had a spouse and two-year-old girl, which concerned Allen.

The chief was about to give the two detectives an assignment that involved danger. He didn't want to bury another family man. Beatty had scored close to the highest Allen had ever seen on the written exam and, likewise, demonstrated prowess at the shooting range. Allen prayed the latter would keep the young man alive.

"Okay, guys," Allen began. "I want you to take this picture of Downing out to Wyoming and show it around. There are two towns on either end of the highway that runs by 'Hell's Half Acre': Casper and Shoshoni ...

"I squeezed our budget to get you the money, and, after humiliating myself in a way no self-respecting officer of the law ought, I persuaded the city council to throw in a bit more ...

"You're both good detectives, so I'll leave it up to you where you circulate the photo. My thinking is that if you get a positive or positives hits, we can be reasonably sure we're close to finding Hamouda and Hainey."

"Boss?"

"Yes, Cam."

"In the manifesto, one of the signers called himself 'Hamouda.' If I'm not mistaken that's an

Arabic name. I think we need to find out if there's a connection between these one percent people and an Arab country. I'm guessing the FBI is also investigating that possibility, but if they aren't ..."

Allen smiled broadly.

"I'd love to get on top of the FBI in any way we can."

"Is there any way we can run the name through various searchable files. I doubt it's a common name, so, if it comes up, we may have some additional clues."

"You see, Peter, that's what new blood or thinking outside the box will do for you!"

Kenmar seemed only slightly chagrined. He'd partnered with Beatty for only a short time, but it had been long enough to gain considerable respect for his intelligence and investigative skills.

*

Two days after the pair of detectives set out for Wyoming, Chief Allen received a staff report on the name 'Hamouda.' There wasn't much to the report, but two entries flashed red. The first, a marriage certificate issued in Detroit for Albert Robinson and Aisha Hamouda in 1981, and the second, an application for food stamps by Aisha Hamouda four years later.

Allen had two questions. One, why no mention of Albert Robinson on the food stamp application, and two, did Aisha need food stamps because she had children to feed? Known originally as 'food stamps,' the Supplemental Nutrition Assistance Program (SNAP) helped people pay for food.

The internal report listed no children, which did not mean Aisha had none, only the possibility that in this case the algorithm made no provision for them. Allen was familiar with the role of computer algorithms in manipulating information in other contexts.

Whether the report listed children was beside the point. All Allen had to do was match the names Robinson and Hamouda with the names on the manifesto (Hamouda-Robinson). He was sure that Albert and Aisha Robinson had a son named Ayman.

Was either parent still living? If so, he or she might have some idea where to find their son. Allen turned to his computer and a Google search for anything related to Albert Robinson or Aisha Hamouda-Robinson.

40

Two large, unsavory-looking men, who seemed capable only of grunting in broken English, ushered 'Frank' and 'Joe'—a.k.a. Billy Roy and Junior—into a modernistic apartment overlooking the Bay and Alcatraz. Had they cared to, they could have watched through two sides of a massive, windowed room as a score of sailboats took advantage of the fresh breezes that were a constant on the Bay. But they were not yachtsmen nor were they there to enjoy the view, as the continued presence of those two large, unsavory characters reminded them.

Instead, they found themselves standing before a man who sat squarely in front of one of those windows finishing what looked to have been a five-course meal. Their deportment would have reminded an imaginary observer of schoolchildren summoned to the principal's office. Dressed impeccably, the diner looked and savored his food as though he were banqueting at a Michelin three-star restaurant.

The seated man picked up his while linen napkin and gently dabbed his thin lips, pretending not to be aware or interested in the presence of 'guests' who continued to stand there, clearly uncomfortable.

The diner's face evidenced the use of Botox and the other fashionable effects inflicted by a plastic surgeon, although the surgeon might have overlooked the need for a collagen injection in those lips. The tight surface of his forehead made more prominent by a receding, wispy hairline of strands once blonde but turning gray, lent to the man's head the character and sheen of a bowling ball.

His facial construct, blue eyes, more the shape of slanted almonds than plump olives, a nose that one could only liken to a ski jump, perhaps the result of an inauspicious boxing career, spoke to his Slavic pedigree. Billy Roy Stewart could hardly stomach looking at the man.

Slouched on a chaise in a corner of the room, a woman, also dressed for that virtual Michelin experience—except for the chewing gum, which mocked any Michelin ambiance. She flipped through the pages of an old copy of *Elle* magazine and, like the diner, paid no mind to the 'guests.' In every way, she evidenced total boredom.

Before he spoke a word, the diner fluttered his napkin at the woman who, without looking at the diner, stopped flipping pages, rose and wordlessly left the room. As there were no other chairs in the room, the walls of which bore evidence of the owner's amateurish appreciation of art (copies of low-brow works), Billy Roy and Junior remained standing.

"Well, gentlemen, you are not here for the view. What have you to report? Unfortunately, my cook only prepared this meal for two. Please forgive me. I had not expected you so soon. So, am I to presume you bring me bad news?"

*

The arrogant speaker was Valery Glebov, familiar to American intelligence—but not Billy Roy and Junior—as an ex-KGB agent in the old Soviet Union who, like his boss in the Kremlin, had eased seamlessly (but not without leaving a few bodies in his wake) into Russia's FSB intelligence service.

Glebov returned his napkin to the table and stared at his 'guests.'

"The question is simple. Is it done?"

"'Smith'?

"Of course!" the diner said impatiently.

"Yes, but I'm afraid the others will be more expensive," Junior volunteered nervously.

Junior's demand took Glebov by surprise, which his expression showed, but it was also Junior's lack of subtlety that challenged the Russian in a way he hadn't experienced before. The pair had done other 'jobs' for Glebov, and both parties believed they understood how the other ticked.

Glebov took a sip of wine. He needed to appear nonplussed to retain the upper hand.

"So, gentlemen"—the word 'gentlemen' oozed out, dripping with sarcasm—he began slowly and with an icy stare, "am I to assume from what you just said that you have thrown in with the American one percent? What a capital idea!"

Glebov smiled at his use of sarcasm and a double entendre.

"So, you see, gentlemen, my English is not so bad. That said, let me warn you never to underestimate *anything* about me."

Neither Billy Roy nor Junior returned the smile, which brought a frown to Glebov's face. The Russian decided he needed to be even more explicit.

"Gentlemen, gentlemen (more oozing). Listen to me very carefully. I'm not sure you understood me when I spoke of underestimation, but your lives depend on grasping the seriousness of everything I say ...

"Leave extortion to the so-called One Percent Gang. It doesn't become you, and you aren't good at it, as even you must realize. So, let us dispense with the disagreeable idea that you will receive a cent more than our original agreement. Have I now made myself clear? It would be most unfortunate for you if I haven't."

The two men looked at each other and shifted their weight from one foot to the other fretfully. It was the second time someone had tried to stiff them, but Glebov was no 'Smith,' and they knew what the Russian meant when he used the word 'unfortunate.' And, of course, there ere those two large, unsavory men.

"Have you found them? Did you squeeze 'Smith' before you ... before he ...?"

"No," Billy Roy interrupted, "we had to do it had before he said anything about their location. He was onto us. He seemed fixated on that Elander woman."

"My, my. You allowed 'Smith' to outwit you, and now you expect me to pay for that mistake and all future bungling. That's quite astonishing, gentlemen. You do understand, of course, there won't be any payment until the job is complete. Is that why you're standing here right now? Because you expected otherwise?"

The two men looked at each other again and shifted their weight from one foot to the other. They had nothing more to say; they knew they had said too much too much already.

"This has become so tiresome. When you leave, gentlemen, which you should have done two minutes ago, please ask the young lady to return. I don't want to see either of you *again* until you have fulfilled the contract. And when you do return, please pick a time that doesn't interfere with my meal. You have given me such an upset stomach. Most unpleasant."

41

Russian President Vladimir Putin had been a KGB agent for 15 years before launching his march to ultimate power in the aftermath of the USSR. His first assignment was to spy on expatriates in St. Petersburg. Next came a posting to the KGB's foreign intelligence division in East Germany, where his job was to identify East Germans—professors, journalists, skilled professionals—to steal intelligence and technology in Western Europe and the United States.

Not everything went as Putin wished; there were events, he discovered, he could not control. As president of the Russian Federation, for example, Putin's expansionist dreams and realities in Georgia, Crimea and Eastern Ukraine made a pariah of Russia in the eyes of the West—again! Cast out of the G8 and G20 economic forums, the Kremlin master concluded Russia could play a meaningful role in world affairs as a disrupter.

*

Enter Valery Glebov. The friendship of Vladimir and Valery began in the good old days of the KGB and Soviet Union. But the empire's dismemberment—the loss of Soviet 'republics' to independence that left behind a stripped-down version of the USSR—and the massive landmass's reduction to a Russian Federation left the country demoralized and ripe for Putin, a czar-like strong man who promised to complete the work of Josef Stalin.

Glebov had joined the KGB in 1966 after he graduated from Leningrad University. The spy agency trained and sent him to the United States to earn a degree in journalism and eventually pose as such in New York. Closer to the aim of the USSR, he was to ingratiate himself to those taking high-level political decisions and to stir the waters.

'Stirring the waters.' Glebov understood the phrase to mean enabling groups like the one percent to tear asunder the economic and political power of the United States at home and abroad. He was to recruit the kind of men who could make sure those divisions flourished by crushing their opponents—in this case the One Percent Gang. The man who had just threatened the lives of two men had for several years been central to Putin's play in the United States.

What would attract men like Billy Roy and Junior to someone like Valery Glebov? Money, of course, the elixir of the espionage game and much, much more. And if an opportunity to exhort more from Glebov presented itself? It would not go well for the would-be extortionists.

The Russians had come late to the game to the game of disruption, late to see their opening, but they were quickly making up for their tardiness.

*

Billy Roy and Junior lied when they told Glebov that 'Bob Smith' hadn't revealed the locations of Ayman and Drew before they gutted him.

'Smith' had tried to save himself. He figured if he told them something, *anything*, they'd buy it and let him go. They wouldn't recognize the truth if it smacked them up the side of the head.

What 'Smith' did say—'Wyoming. Somewhere in Wyoming'—was so vague, so absurd Stewart and Phillips dared not even hint to Glebov they knew anything.

'Smith' had tried to make it sound matter of fact, as though by sounding nonplussed, not panicky, he would be convincing. Not hedging. Not worried he would appear to be lying.

But it was too late. 'Wyoming. Somewhere in Wyoming' turned out to be his final words. From the moment he sat down in that Rendezvous booth, it was too late.

*

Valery Glebov, like his counterintelligence buddy, Putin, could not tolerate insubordination, failure or opposition. All-powerful men like Glebov and Putin were quite absurd. They lived in fear, which meant they were as naked as the emperor of the allegory and dependent on thugs, not persuasion, for their legitimacy. Fear and thuggery were fundamental to the psychology of power politics, which Stewart and Phillips, had they thought ahead, might have kept in mind as a matter of their survival. Everyone under the thumb of Valery Glebov or Vladimir Putin lived on borrowed time.

Stewart and Phillips—like most thugs selected by all-powerful men but not the dimmest bulbs in the room—might gut someone in a booth at the Rendezvous and still not realize sharpened knives would come for them.

42

Brian Downing's failure to communicate left Hamouda and Hainey cut off from each other and the world. Without Downing, the Arco duo had lost their ability to direct attacks on the one percent. It was a contingency for which they had failed to plan. They had no idea why he hadn't maintained their established communication schedule, and both had the same thoughts. Had the police caught him? Had he turned on them?

Two weeks had passed and neither Hamouda nor Hainey had heard from Downing. Independently, one of them, possibly both, considered leaving their semi-secret locations to confirm what they feared: the police had Downing. If so, they needed to consider retreating to the underground bunker or somehow finding a new messenger. For their protection and the direction of surrogates, they needed someone to travel back and forth. That was still their only means of communication with each other, a safety protocol they considered essential.

Drew Hainey decided to act. As a postal clerk, he was in the best position of the two to monitor the FBI's most wanted listings and search newspapers for any clue about Downing. First, however, he believed he needed to check if Ayman had sensed the danger suggested by Downing's failure to report and had already retreated to their underground bunker.

*

Three days after leaving Sausalito Peter Kenmar and Cameron Beatty sat drinking coffee in the Cowboy Café in DuBois, Wyoming.

"I don't know where to begin, Cam. This is a big, empty state. If the guys we're looking for are here, it could be damn hard to find them ...

"On the plus side, though, we have one location of interest—'Hell's Half Acre.' Let's go back to that motel we passed just before getting into town, get a room and spend some time going over the map of Wyoming and see if we can make sense of what the Chief told us about this abandoned resort. It's a guess at best, but it's all we have."

*

Billy Roy and Junior were as blind as the two detectives. They, too, had only one clue: 'Somewhere in Wyoming,' 'Bob Smith's' last words. In their minds, a man's last words had to be meaningful. So, the pair had flown to Casper and rented a car, as did two other men a day later.

Valery Glebov wasn't particular about the character of the men he hired. Among those arrested and sent to jails and prisons in the United States were some the FSB had turned to identify and recruit disenchanted prisoners nearing their parole dates for service to men like Glebov. Recent among such recruits were a couple of small-time drug traffickers, Billy Roy, Phillips and two others, Ed Swoveland and Eugene ('Gene') Thomas, with rap sheets that included burglary, assault and attempted rape.

Years earlier, Billy Roy Stewart and Junior Phillips came of age in the rough-and-tumble shipyards of Pascagoula Mississippi. There, they met seamen from places they may have dreamed of but would never see, some exotic, most of them not. The hard, demanding work with steel plates developed their bodies and reputations as tough, sometimes violent men who knew how to take orders and keep their mouths shut.

Poverty, broken families and early gang membership had also selected, honed and sharpened both for the unpleasant but lucrative jobs that eventually drew them to men like Valery Glebov. In turn, the Russian moved toward them with a sinister, inexorable intensity and, in the tradition of Doktor Faustus (Johann Georg Faust), offered them riches beyond imagination in return for ...

Swoveland and Thomas's backgrounds (poverty, broken homes, arrests for petty and not so petty crimes, violence, toughness) differed little from the Pascagoula steel men, except the location: Los Angeles. In its mission to undermine American society from within, the FSB had little difficulty recruiting such men.

*

Brian Downing's failure to contact the Arco duo left each man blind as to the location and plan of the other. Take Drew Hainey. He drove his pickup from Shoshoni north to Thermopolis and the hotel he remembered as Ayman's last residence. Unable to find his partner, he had to assume the police had caught up with him, as perhaps they had Brian, or that Ayman had already retreated to their bunker. Should he go there as well? He still had no idea why Brian Downing hadn't come to Shoshoni, either with a message from Ayman or to pass along his thoughts to his partner. Drew Hainey left Thermopolis for 'Hell's Half Acre.'

Hainey's theory about Ayman was partially true. Downing's disappearance had alarmed Hamouda, and he decided that rather than retreat to an uncomfortable life underground for an extended period, he would simply move north to another Wyoming town: Worland.

*

"Cam, this map doesn't indicate there's much between Shoshoni and Casper. It does, however, still show the location of 'Hell's Half Acre.' That's the place Big Mike told me about."

"So, what do you propose?"

"I think we need to have a look at that abandoned resort ... try to figure out why Allen thought it important."

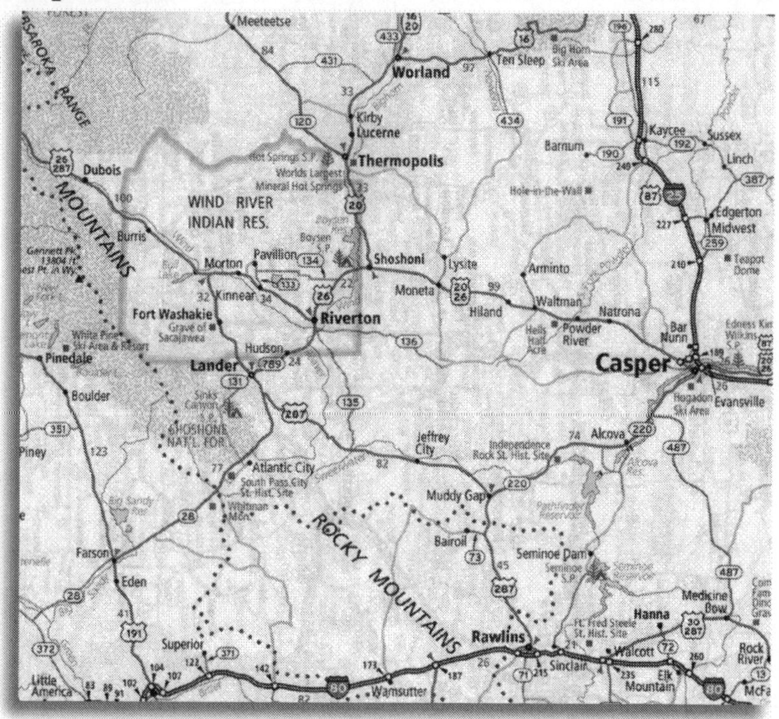

"I agree. We'll drive over there first thing in the morning. If we don't find anything of relevance there, we go on to Casper, call the chief and see what he wants us to do next."

It took most of the next day for the two detectives to drive to 'Hell's Half Acre.' There wasn't much to see, only the foundations and some above-ground remnants of what they assumed to have been the old motel and restaurant. It's always difficult to imagine that buildings, now torn down, once sat in such small spaces. Vertical structures deceive the brain's ability to account for the true horizontal space those buildings once occupied.

What appeared to have been a parking lot lay behind the motel and restaurant. The perimeter of the lot, delineated by a dilapidated hurricane fence topped by barbed wire, appeared irregular, perhaps 50 yards across at the rear and at the sides, 25 by 35 yards. The land beyond the back fence dropped off, suggesting the edge of a cliff.

Drawn by the sight of an a nine or ten-year-old Ford 150 near the rear fence, they drove through a half-opened gate, which moved from side to side on rollers, just wide enough for a car or truck. The gate had fallen off its rollers in a cockeyed slant and inward lean that suggested a slight push would send the entire apparatus crashing to the ground.

The two detectives proceeded through the gap in the gate into the gravel-covered lot and stopped. The space in front of them was mostly empty except for the pickup and leftover construction material stacked haphazardly near the fencing—cinder blocks, broken lumber, porcelain fixtures and rusted metal—used either when the restaurant and motel functioned or in their demolition.

"What do you think, Peter?"

"Looks like someone junked their old truck and left it for someone else to get rid of, like all the rest of the crap. Let's walk around a bit and see if there's anything of interest, anything else that looks like it doesn't belong, even here."

*

The nine or ten-year-old Ford 150, which any objective observer would have concluded didn't belong, drew Kenmar and Beatty like moths to the flame, putting their proposed walk-around on hold.

43

'Somewhere in Wyoming.' 'Bob Smith's' last words. It was next to nothing to go on, but Stewart and Phillips had to make *something* of it.

"I've been studyin' this map of the state, Billy. What I see are towns and cities around the edges and a lot of nothing in the middle. But look at that middle. It's interesting. There's a circle of highways surrounding it. U.S. 287 on the south connects Lander and Casper by way of Jeffrey City and Alcova, and U.S. 20/26 at the top of the circle does the same by way of Riverton and Shoshoni."

"Yeah, and if it was me and I was trying to make myself scarce, I'd go for that dead space in the circle and I'd still have highways all around me to get in and out when I needed to."

"Okay, but where and how would you hide in that dead space? We don't even know what the terrain's like there."

"Well, we're not going to find out sittin' on our fat, lazy a**es in this motel!"

"So, what do you propose?"

"We drive the circle and check it out. Look for some place, any place, those bozos might hide. Take 287 over to Lander, stay overnight, and then return here on 20/26. I think we'll need at least two days if we're gonna check out the terrain here and there."

*

Something in his peripheral vision got Cameron's attention as it moved suddenly from sunlight into the shadow underneath the nine or ten-year-old Ford 150. A snake? A 'prairie dog'?

Ground squirrel? Gila Monster? He wasn't sure, but his boredom turned to curiosity. He bent down to look under the truck and saw something out of place. He went to his hands and knees to get an even better look.

"Come and take a look at this, Peter."

"Whaddya got, Cam?"

"I don't know. I was having trouble staying engaged when something moving on the ground caught my eye. I got down and tried to see what it was, and that's when I saw something fishy. You see that steel plate under there?"

Kenmar went to his hands and knees.

"Yes."

"Look carefully. It's only half covered with dirt, like someone had swept it or the dirt jarred loose for some reason."

"You got that small flashlight you always carry?"

"Yeah, here you go."

Most small flashlights, including the one Beatty just handed his partner, had incredibly bright beams. For example, the Fenix and Surefire lights shined over 200 lumens and were extremely useful at night.

Kenmar shined the light underneath the chassis, satisfied himself that his partner was right about the plate and stood.

"It's not only that plate, Cam, so be prepared for anything."

"What do you mean, Peter?"

"Before you drew my attention under the truck, I had put my hand on the hood. No reason. Just to touch it, I suppose. Sort of an instinct when I'm around a vehicle. Good thing I did. *The hood was still warm!* Someone ran that engine, maybe drove it, just before we arrived."

*

He heard the steps and then the voices. Drew Hainey quietly retrieved an AR-15 that lay on one of the remaining dusty bus seats. His heart racing, he crouched behind a seat back and trained his rifle at the ladder.

44

Ayman Hamouda faced the same quandary as had Drew Hainey. With no Downing and no communication with his partner, he had grown antsy. Before executing his end of their emergency plan, he had decided to move to Worland. He was confident that eventually the safest place for him would be the underground bus, where he believed no one would ever find them. But Ayman was also a practical man, a man like most men—although most men were not hunted—who wasn't anxious to rush from a normal, above ground life into an underground bunker for an extended period.

*

Detective Beatty slid underneath the pickup toward the steel plate. The circumstance seemed extraordinary. Ominous. He sensed that if he touched that plate his world would change forever. There would be no going back. But he was a policeman, and right now it was his job to touch that plate, to move it if he could.

He was a soldier whose team and its mission depended on him no matter how scared he might be. He had to touch that plate for them, not for himself, not for country and certainly not for apple pie and Chevrolet or any of the other phony baloney patriotism that people might throw at him. So, he tried to move the plate but found its weight and his lack of leverage inadequate. He slid back out.

"It's going to take both of us to move that plate, Peter."

"You think it's covering something, not just another piece of junk like we've seen all over this lot?"

"Why would someone deliberately stop a truck on top of that plate unless they were trying to hide it?"

"Okay, I agree. It's worth a try to move it."

This time both men slid under the pickup and positioned themselves at diagonal corners. Gradually, the plate began to move, centimeter by centimeter, until it revealed the opening of a hole.

Suddenly, the business end of a rifle barrel emerged from the hole and fired a half-dozen rounds. The bullets hit no one, but the sound of the gas explosions and ricochets off the bottom of the truck chassis caused both detectives to cover their ears and scootch as quickly as they could from under the truck and run zigzag toward their own vehicle for cover.

"Jesus H. Christ!" Kenmar yelled as bullets clanged off their vehicle. "Here we are in the middle of nowhere with no backup. Go around to the trunk and get me something besides my Glock. There should be a 12 gauge and a .45 ... And get our vests. Stay low, goddammit!"

*

"Hey!" Junior yelled. "Stop! Look over there!"

"At what?"

"Two guys behind a car over there are firing at a pickup next to that fence. Oh, s**t! Someone is firing back."

"Maybe this is what Glebov wanted us to deal with."

"Yeah, but who's who? Who are we supposed to deal with? Which vehicle?"

"Gimme those binoculars. There's someone under that pickup. Looks like he's in a hole. I can only see his head. No body."

"That's got to be our guy. The others must be cops."

"We got to get rid of the cops first, otherwise we never get to our guys. Back up. Over there behind that slight rise. You see it?"

"Yeah, yeah, I'm doin' it."

When Billy Roy had finished parking, both men exited their vehicle with weapons drawn, including an AR-15 in Junior's hands, and ran in a crouch toward a pile of rubble in the remains of the motel/restaurant. As soon as they flopped down into prone positions, they opened fire on the rear of Kenmar and Beatty.

45

Ed Swoveland and Gene Thomas had been shadowing Billy Roy and Junior since all four left separately from Casper. Following was both tedious and boring. The trailing pair had no idea, of course, what Stewart and Phillips were doing ... except driving. Occasionally, the lead vehicle slowed or stopped. When the latter occurred, Swoveland and Thomas had no choice but to pass and wait on a side road ahead, as much out of sight as possible, before resuming pursuit.

That routine suited none of the four. They were muscle men, action men, gunmen, not detectives or thinkers. Certainly not men to sit around in cars all day watching the vast nothingness of Wyoming sweep by without a clue regarding their objective.

*

Back in the Bay Area, Valery Glebov had his hands full fielding calls, first from Billy Roy and Junior and then Swoveland and Thomas. Obviously, when issuing orders, he had to be careful not to mistake the identity and purpose of one car for those of the other. Stewart and Phillips were after the One Percent Gang; Ed and Gene were to eliminate Billy Roy and Junior after the Gang. Presumably, then, the one percent element would be free to do Putin's work. Glebov's was a delicate and complicated dance.

*

It was about to become even more complicated. Special Agent Tom Wilson may have suggested to Chief Allen that the Bureau was taking a hands-off position regarding Allen's investigation of the multiple murders that had occurred since Robert and Emily Lansing, but Wilson was no fool. He had no intention of allowing a Sausalito police department free rein to do his work.

So, a parade of vehicles would descend on an unsuspecting Wyoming, three carloads of determined men, either police or gangsters, *plus* Special Agent Tom Wilson and one of his agents in a fourth vehicle which had been following Kenmar and Beatty. Wilson was old school when it came to weaponry, and he was taking no chances. The trunk of his government car held an AR-15 and his personal M60, vintage Vietnam, and Thompson submachinegun ... a.k.a. 'Tommy Gun.'

Wilson's air-cooled M60 had a muzzle velocity of 2,800 feet per second. He could hold it and fire from the hip (not likely), although it weighed 23 pounds (soldiers in Vietnam called it 'the pig'). Preferably, he could fire it from its built-in bipod or mounted on a tripod for accuracy at longer ranges.

The M60 had a conspicuous role in Vietnam during the 1960s and 70s but was no longer part of the U.S. military's inventory. Nonetheless, it remained one of the most valued items in any machine-gun collection. What use Wilson intended for it in Wyoming, if any, remained to be seen. Certainly, no one wanted to be on the receiving end of any of Agent Wilson's arsenal.

*

Swoveland and Thomas, who had stopped for a bathroom break, had lost sight of Billy Roy and Junior. Bored, tired and clueless they approached 'Hell's Half Acre' at high speed, trying to regain sight of the leading car.

"S**t! There they are! Stop!"

Swoveland brought the car to a halt but had to back up to see what Thomas yelled about.

"My God, they're shooting at someone! But who?"

"And the 'someone' ... There are two of them behind that pile of rubble," Ed added, "are shooting at that car. What the hell?"

"If its cops they're firing at, we gotta help 'em out. Then we deal with their futures."

Gene Thomas pulled up next to Billy Roy and Junior's car and exited in a crouch with their weapons.

"Who the f**k are you guys?" Junior said, turning toward the newcomers who had just flopped down next to he and Billy Roy.

"Are those cops out there?" Thomas asked without answering Junior.

"We assume so."

"Then we're here to help," Swoveland answered. "Who's the guy under that pickup?"

By now, Stewart had become suspicious. He didn't know Swoveland or Thomas, and he didn't want to answer the question. He did wonder, of course, who the new arrivals were and why they happened along at the precise moment of the confrontation with the cops and the guy under the nine or ten-year-old Ford 150.

Kenmar and Beatty, under enfiladed fire, had retreated to their vehicle. The attack on them was so intense they curled up on the floor, ending their ability to return fire. Above them, bullets shredded their vehicle.

*

The four Glebov mercenaries, focused so intently and exclusively on Kenmar and Beatty, failed to notice the arrival of the fourth vehicle.

"FBI! Cease fire and drop your weapons! Do it! Now!"

But the firing continued. Tom Wilson could see a vehicle rock from bullet impacts, and he assumed it must be the detective's. He realized that if Mike Allen's guys were still alive, and he feared it likely they were not since he saw no return fire, they had little or no chance of survival.

"FBI! Cease firing and drop your weapons!" He shouted again.

The sound of continuing weapon discharges drowned out Wilson's commands. Then, Gene Thomas did something good sense should have prevented.

He looked behind him to find another magazine for his AR and saw someone about 50 yards away holding up what he took to be a badge. He grabbed the magazine, locked it in place and pointed his weapon at the man holding the badge. It was the last thing he ever did.

A spray from Tom Wilson's M60 cut Thomas in half. His gore showered the other three, who collectively made the same mistake as Thomas. They turned around and opened fire on the two FBI agents. The M60 ended their assault on law enforcement as well.

Peter Kenmar and Cameron Beatty realized the heavy fire on them had stopped, but the person in the hole under the nine or ten-year-old Ford 150 hadn't. And then it did. The relieved pair of detectives watched in astonishment as something shredded that Ford 150, rolling it onto its side and exposing the hole.

"Cover us!" yelled one of the two men who had rushed to what remained of the detective's vehicle. As the new pair moved cautiously toward the hole, Kenmar noticed the bright yellow letters on the backs of their blue jackets: **FBI**.

46

Unnoticed by those preoccupied with involvement in the desperate gunfight in the parking lot, a fifth car arrived at the unfolding slaughter.

Before Ayman Hamouda fled from his Worland hotel, he had grabbed whatever food and water remained, a 9mm handgun, an AR-15-stryle assault rifle and ammunition for both weapons. He descended the fire escape's ladder to the alley, climbed into his RAM 1500 and drove out of town to U.S. 20 south to Shoshoni. When he did not find Hainey at his hotel, he concluded his partner had fled to the underground bunker. He left town on U.S. 20/26 for 'Hell's Half Acre.'

'Stay calm,' he told himself repeatedly as he drove. He went over in his mind what he'd do when he got there, depending on the situation. Two and a half hours later what he'd do wasn't a mystery.

Ayman Hamouda rolled slowly by the site of the former resort. He drew the obvious conclusion from what he saw—the end of the One Percent Gang.

Ayman increased his speed gradually so as not to draw attention to his presence. What he'd seen gave him plenty to think about. How had they found Drew? He was either dead or if still alive interrogated harshly without regard for his rights. If the latter, would Drew give up his partner under pressure?

'Where should I hide now?'

He tried to think how he might stay a step or two ahead of the law, but it was difficult in his current, panic-stricken moment.

*

Minutes earlier Kenmar and Beatty had opened fire at the hole as instructed by Tom Wilson, and the FBI men, bent low, rushed forward, Wilson armed with his Tommy Gun.' When they reached the rolled over Ford 150 and took cover behind it, Wilson yelled at his partner.

"Gimme me that concussion grenade!"

Bill Stuart handed it over. Wilson pulled the pin and tossed it into the hole. Both men ducked and covered their ears.

As the smoke and dust began to dissipate, Bill Stuart crawled to the hole and peered down. Drew Hainey lay at the foot of the ladder.

Stuart signaled all clear to Wilson, and both men descended into the bus. Wilson cuffed Hainey, who was still alive but disoriented.

"Just look at this place, Bill. Somebody went to a lot of trouble to hide, but what good did it do them?"

Hainey began to stir and Wilson began his interrogation, beginning by citing his Miranda rights.

"Do you understand your rights as I have explained them?"

Drew nodded.

"Name?"

"F**k you, man."

"Okay, have it your way, but I can assure you it won't be something you'll enjoy. We'll find out who you are when we get your prints, so, you should consider cooperating now."

*

While the FBI men were in the bus, Kenmar and Beatty rushed to the other four who were badly torn up by that M60. Ed Swoveland alone among them was still breathing, but Peter could tell it wouldn't be long.

"Cam, get on 911 and call for an ambulance. Tell 'em we've got multiple KIA and wounded."

"Where do I tell 'em we are?"

"Not sure. Just say we're about 40 miles west of Casper on Highways 20/26 at a place that's been demolished."

"Who sent you?" Peter pressed Swoveland.

"Water," he croaked. "Water ..."

"No water. It'll kill you. Tell me who sent you."

Swoveland, who was in no condition to appreciate Kenmar's irony, swallowed hard, which forced more bubbling blood out of the side of his chest torn open by the M60.

Kenmar watched the man's laborious breathing. Clearly, he hadn't the strength to speak up. But the man beckoned weakly—more like a twitch—with his left index finger. The detective bent down and put his ear close to Swoveland's bloody lips.

"Russia," Kenmar was sure he had whispered. "Russian ... Glebov ... Russ ..."

Then his head lolled to one side, and his open eyes stared but saw nothing.

47

Valery Glebov hadn't heard from either of his clean-up teams. He had to assume the worst, not their deaths but the likely prospect they were alive and talking.

As an FSB agent, he operated surreptitiously in the Bay Area without diplomatic protection. He was smart enough and practiced enough to realize the FBI and American counterintelligence would eventually be at his door; he was also wily enough to know how to slip out of the country.

*

Tom Wilson knew the name, 'Glebov,' and believed he was a step or two ahead of the Russian who, he assumed, would not know that he, Wilson, was onto him. He persuaded FBI headquarters in Washington to issue an APB, which included the Russian's photograph and a list of known aliases. The query also put public transportation—buses, railways, shipping and air—on full alert.

It was all for naught. The BBC and FOX News broadcast a meeting between Vladimir Putin and Valery Glebov less than a week after the shootout at 'Hell's Half Acre.' The BBC showed a silent Putin in an ornate Kremlin room, seated at one end of a long table length at the other from Glebov. Both were full of bonhomie, the Kremlin boss presumably congratulating his old pal on the success of his efforts to stymie the One Percent Gang.

When it became Glebov's turn to speak, the sound came on, and in passable English (translated on the screen for Russian viewers) he lashed out at the 'anti-social, reactionary forces' in the

United States and named the One Percent Gang in particular.

The whole performance was an astonishing departure from the Kremlin's century-old, anti-capitalist philosophy, its *raison d'être*. But Putin, ever the shifty pragmatist, had discovered another way of attacking the United States: foment internal dissention, help—encourage—the one percent to run wild regardless of ideology.

Putin had another advantage beside the cowering Glebov. He was a master of stagecraft, and he had complete control of the tool he needed to keep himself in power: television. In the 1970s and 1980s, television became the Soviet Union's preeminent mass medium. Just before the collapse of the regime and its empire in 1989, an estimated 93 percent of the population watched television. When Vladimir Putin captured the government, he also gained control of a vast audience for his propaganda.

No one heard from or of Valery Glebov again. The fastidious diner vanished from public view without a trace, except, perhaps, in the meticulous records maintained about the unfortunate souls condemned to the gulag. His was the inevitable fate of a man who knew too much in Putin's Soviet-style state.

*

Closer to the United States and patterned after Russia, the Cuban government—the Communist Party of Cuba—owned and operated all Cuban media, including the national TV channels.

One day after the Moscow broadcast, Cuban television aired an interview in Havana between Ayman Hamouda and Cuban president, Miguel Díaz-Canel. The essence of the broadcast mimicked—up to a point—Putin's staged show, a clear indication the Kremlin still called the tune in Cuba.

But the carefully choreographed, anti-capitalist interview did not celebrate the guest. Instead, Diaz-Canel repeatedly chastised Hamouda. *El Presidenté*'s guest,' who appeared shackled, may have imagined the Castro brother's successor would welcome him, but his trip to the island gulag proved anything but pleasant.

Days after his celebrated interview with the island's president, Ayman Hamouda reportedly disappeared from his Cuban version of a Russian dacha. Speculation in the capital among those who knew of Hamouda's defection held that *El Presidenté*, in a move that one could only view as the height of irony, had the gringo anti-capitalist taken into the jungle and shot.

The president, perhaps unfamiliar with the sense of irony found in the English language, let associates announce that he, *El Presidenté*, wanted nothing to do with such a cold-blooded killer who, if he remained on the island, would give it a bad name!

*

The state of Wyoming extradited Drew Hainey to California to face multiple charges, including extortion, assaulting a police officer, resisting arrest, solicitation of murder and conspiracy to commit murder. His public defender laid out a trial strategy but cautioned his client he faced daunting odds. When he told Hainey about his partner's interview with *El Presidenté,* his face fell.

After a three-week trial, during which the defendant either sulked like a scolded schoolboy or lashed out verbally at the district attorney and judge, a jury convicted him on all charges and the judge sentenced him to. At his sentencing (life in prison without parole), the judge told Hainey, repeatedly overruling loud and fulsome objections from Hainey's public defender, that he would have given him the death penalty had that option been available.

*

Special Agent Tom Wilson remained with the Bureau and reached a sort of celebratory status—as much as one could in the FBI—when his continued investigation of the One Percent Gang led to arrests throughout the state and the end of the once sprawling, murderous empire of Drew Hainey and Ayman Hamouda.

*

The University of Michigan expunged the honors and degrees the partners had achieved. Hamouda and Hainey had instructed Mr. 'Smith' to have Rebecca Elander erased as though she never existed. Now, Mr. 'Smith' was dead and they? In a word, erased.

*

What had the 'Robin Hood Solution' accomplished? Almost nothing. There were those in Congress sympathetic to the goals of the manifesto, but not enough of them.

There had always been those among the public and in Congress who took plight of the Palestinians seriously and fought for the goals that Ayman Hamouda would have applauded. But they were too few and insufficiently motivated to exert the kind of pressure on Israel that would make a difference.

*

Big Mike Allen served out the remainder of the term he had agreed to when Sausalito's mayor picked him out of the force, and then he retired. In private, his wife and friends explained to the curious that the One Percent Gang's spree had robbed Mike, once a boisterous and loud patriot, of any positive regard he had for human nature and the efficacy of law enforcement.

*

The One Percent Gang took a toll on two other policemen. Cameron Beatty joined the FBI. A few months later, after only a short time in the field, he died in another gunfight, ambushed when local police and Bureau agents moved in on another of the Gang's tentacles in Bakersfield, California.

Peter Kenmar's recent experiences in gun-fights taught him two things: he could be gone in the wink of an eye, having made little or no dent in crime; and life *must* offer something better. It did.

Kenmar began a romantic relationship with Rebecca Elander. He left the Sausalito Police Department and she the Bank of Marin. They married and moved to Humboldt County—he the prodigal son—and began raising a family on the dairy farm Peter took over from his father. Of course, this brought smile after to smile to Jessie Kenmar's face.

*

Finally, Vladimir Putin. As with all those of his ilk, someone would eventually come to his door with a sharpened knife. One supposes he's familiar enough with Russian and Soviet history to know it and would have it no other way.

DEBTS

As with all my stories, my principal debt is to my wife, Sheila Ross. It always pleases me to say this, although the expression of it alone does not account for the sum of my gratitude.

For this book, instead of her quietly reading it to herself, I read it aloud. We discussed various elements of the developing manuscript after each session and at meals. She pulled me back repeatedly from the metaphorical brink of one of those ravines at 'Hell's Half Acre' and offered sensible suggestions for the manuscript's improvement.

*

I relied on Wikipedia for several topics: dimethyl sulfide (DMS) and Almai; venture capitalism; the Roosevelt's political quotations; the Richmond Shipyards; NI-BRS; Arco, Idaho; the Parnall Correctional Facility; the 'Renewed Declaration of Independence,'; the Fiskhorn and Poletown East neighborhoods of Detroit; 'Operation Wrath of God'; Wyoming Dinosaurs; 'Hell's Half Acre' (visited on my bicycle); Shoshoni; Combined DNA Index System (CODIS); 'Mickey Finn'; the M60; and Russian and Cuban media.

I rode my bicycle from DuBois to Torrington, Wyoming, which included the stretch from Shoshoni to Hell's Half Acre, where I was fortunate to get enough food at the restaurant to fuel me on to Casper.

Ultimately, the accuracy of everything in these pages is my responsibility.

AUTHOR

Stephen Carey Fox is a Navy veteran of the Vietnam Era and Emeritus Professor of History at Humboldt State University (now Cal Poly Humboldt). His teaching career there spanned four decades.

He is the author of award-winning articles and book-length oral/documentary histories of the relocation and internment of Europeans of enemy nationality in the United States during World

War II. His work helped to re-kindle scholarly and popular interest in the topic.

Steve turned to fiction for the pleasure of 'telling lies for fun.' His books consider crime—especially crime—history, feminism, reminiscence, family, and contemporary political, economic and social issues.

He writes from behind northern California's 'Redwood Curtain' in Willow Creek, a village renowned as the home of Sasquatch (a.k.a. Bigfoot) and 'medicinal gardens.'

Made in the USA
Columbia, SC
11 August 2024